She smiled a little. "everything."

"Yeah, I guess." He said it slowly, at the last moment looking at her lips before lifting his gaze to her eyes again.

Chloe swallowed hard. Before she did something stupid, something she couldn't take back, she broke eye contact and stepped around him.

"I need to check how well your incisions are healing." Though the thought of looking at even that little sliver of skin caused heat to flood her cheeks. As least her back was to him. Without waiting for Wyatt, she headed to her bedroom and pulled fresh bandages from the bag she'd stored there.

When she turned around, Wyatt was almost done unbuttoning his shirt. "What are you doing?"

He paused. "Taking it off."

"You don't have to do that."

"I'm not going to sleep in it." He smiled as he slipped the last two buttons through the holes and shrugged out of the shirt.

Her mouth went dry, and she was probably staring at him as if she'd never seen a half-naked man before.

Still smiling, Wyatt crossed the space between them. "Do I make you nervous, Dr. Brody?"

Dear Reader,

Welcome back to Blue Falls, Texas, a town that has become so real to me that I want to go shopping at the Yesterwear Boutique, eat pastries at the Mehlerhaus Bakery and go for a walk around Blue Falls Lake. Oh, and let's not forget having a good time at one of the local rodeos filled with cowboys with rodeo in their blood.

It's one of those rodeos that brings my latest hero, Wyatt Kelley, to Blue Falls. And the injury he sustains when he's thrown from a bull is what brings him into Dr. Chloe Brody's emergency room...and into her heart.

I tend to write stories about people who have endured loss but find a way to move on and fall in love. This couldn't be more true for Wyatt and Chloe, and I hope you enjoy reading their story as much as I enjoyed writing it.

Trish Milburn

THE DOCTOR'S COWBOY

—

Trish Milburn

Recycling programs
for this product may
not exist in your area.

ISBN-13: 978-0-373-75559-2

The Doctor's Cowboy

Printed in U.S.A.

™ www.Harlequin.com

Trish Milburn writes contemporary romance for the Harlequin American Romance line and paranormal romance for the Harlequin Nocturne series. She's a two-time Golden Heart Award winner, a fan of walks in the woods and road trips, and a big geek girl, including being a dedicated Whovian and Browncoat. And from her earliest memories, she's been a fan of Westerns, be they historical or contemporary. There's nothing quite like a cowboy hero.

Books by Trish Milburn

Harlequin American Romance

A Firefighter in the Family
Her Very Own Family
The Family Man
Elly: Cowgirl Bride
The Texan's Cowgirl Bride

The Teagues of Texas

The Cowboy's Secret Son
Cowboy to the Rescue
The Cowboy Sheriff

Blue Falls, Texas

Her Perfect Cowboy
Having the Cowboy's Baby
Marrying the Cowboy

Visit the Author Profile page
at Harlequin.com for more titles

Thanks to San Dee Keefner for her help with the medical/ER aspects of this story.

And to all the readers of the Blue Falls, Texas books who have written to me about enjoying the stories or who have left lovely reviews online, thank you so much!

Chapter One

Wyatt Kelley stood on the edge of the bucking chute, looking down at the monster bull. Beelzebub. From what he'd heard of the bull's nasty attitude, the demonic name fit. Yeah, this had "easy ride" written all over it. The moment he mounted the two-ton bull, ol' Beezy let him know exactly what he thought of having a rider by twitching, fidgeting, snorting. Basically saying, "Your butt is toast."

"I don't think he wants to be your best friend," said one of the cowboys manning the chute.

"What?" Wyatt patted the bull on the side of his neck. "This little guy is a sweetheart. We're going out for drinks afterward."

As if to disagree, Beezy stomped the dirt and shuddered beneath him, causing the bell hanging from the lower part of Wyatt's bull rope to clang.

"Next up, we've got a cowboy out of the Cowboy State," the rodeo announcer said as Wyatt readjusted the rope, getting his grip just right. "Wyatt Kelley will be riding Beelzebub."

Wyatt took a deep breath, let it out, then nodded. The moment the chute opened, Beelzebub shot out and began bucking as if Wyatt were a nest full of angry hornets. The arena around him became a dirt-brown blur as the bull spun and kicked so hard it nearly jarred the teeth out of Wyatt's head. As if ticked off that he hadn't gotten rid of Wyatt's weight yet, Beezy switched directions and kicked even harder.

Wyatt held on for all he was worth, pretty sure this was the longest eight seconds of his career. And he'd ridden more bulls than he could count. In the next moment, his hat went flying. Sensing victory, the bull seemed to corral all of his intense power and did a belly roll, coming completely off the ground as he kicked all four feet out to the side. Wyatt felt himself slide but he tightened his hold on the rope and his legs pressed against the bull's sides. By some miracle, he stayed on.

But as soon as the bull landed on his feet, he went into a spin that spelled doom. In less than the blink of an eye, the bull bucked Wyatt off into the well, the center of the rank bastard's spin. Wyatt's heart rate accelerated when he realized his hand was caught in his rope, adrenaline fueling panic. He fought to free himself, but before he could Beezy caught him with a horn.

Pain shot through the lower part of his side just before he went airborne and was flung to the other side of the bull. Wyatt was still fighting to free himself and not succumb to the pain when the bull caught him again, this time across his abdomen just below his safety vest.

This was not good. Really not good.

Wyatt felt like a rag doll, one that might well soon have its guts spilling over the dirt of the arena. It wasn't as if he hadn't thought of dying like this before, but the reality sure did suck a bushel of lemons.

His body slammed against the ground before he realized his hand had finally come loose from the rope.

His vision dimmed, and he didn't think he could move even if he saw the bull's hooves heading toward his face. But it wasn't the bull that came into his line of sight but rather the painted face of one of the bull-fighters.

"Hang on, buddy." The man's words sounded off, as if they were having to move through water or maybe thick syrup to reach Wyatt's ears. "We're going to get you some help."

The bullfighter shifted away to speak to someone Wyatt couldn't see. Wyatt stared up at the sky beyond the lights of the arena and blinked slowly. He wondered if he looked down would he find that the lower half of his body was no longer attached to the top half and they just hadn't told him yet.

He wasn't sure how much time passed, but it seemed between one blink and the next paramedics appeared. He glanced to the right and saw an ambulance. At least it wasn't a hearse. Guess that meant he wasn't dead. They fitted him with a neck brace without too much trouble. But when they started to slip a backboard beneath him, he cried out without even thinking about it. That tended to happen when it felt as if your gut were being sliced open with a flaming hot machete.

In the next moment, the two paramedics and what must have been half the cowboys in attendance were lifting him and carrying him to the ambulance. Somehow the muffled applause of the spectators reached him, and the guy from the chute smiled down at him.

"Hear that? You're going to get a lot of ladies after this."

Wyatt wasn't entirely sure that the body parts that would interest the ladies weren't long gone. And when they loaded him in the ambulance, causing a fresh hell to tear at his middle, thoughts of the ladies were the furthest thing from his mind.

Everything seemed to send a new shock wave of pain through him. The slamming shut of the ambulance door, the driver climbing into the front seat, the jouncing of the rig as it left the arena. When the ambulance made the turn out of the rodeo grounds onto the road, black dots appeared in front of Wyatt's eyes.

"To hell with this," he thought before letting himself pass out.

DR. CHLOE BRODY dropped the coins into the snack machine then looked through the glass front at her choices. The granola bar or bag of apple slices were the wisest choices, but the chocolate cupcakes seemed to be singing a siren song to her. *Come on, you know you want to*, that devious package of sugary goodness whispered. *You can run off the pesky calories later.*

Giving in to temptation, she punched the appropriate buttons and watched the cupcakes drop.

"Hey, Doc," called Lori Dalton from the ER nurses' station. "You want to enter the pool?"

Chloe grabbed her cupcakes and walked toward the trio of women behind the desk. "I'm afraid to ask. What's the pool for?"

Sophie Wells, a petite blonde, looked up and smiled. "On who Verona is going to target next."

Chloe laughed as she leaned against the wall that separated the nurses' station from the four curtained trauma and triage areas. Verona Charles was Blue Falls's version of Cupid. Her favorite pastime was seeing which couples she could match up. While she sent many happily single people fleeing, she did have a remarkably good rate of success. Last year alone, she'd not only successfully matched her niece, Elissa, but also Elissa's two best friends, India and Skyler. And she'd probably had her hand in a few more couples ending up together.

"You all are tempting fate," Chloe said.

"I already have a man," said Lori as she flashed her engagement ring.

Chloe gestured toward Sophie and Jenna Marks, who normally worked at the clinic with Chloe but was picking up some extra hours at the hospital. As usual, the nurse had her dark brown hair pulled back in a thick ponytail that swayed when she moved. "Yeah, but these two don't."

"Well, you could help with Jenna," Sophie said. "She's had the hots for your brother forever."

Jenna swatted Sophie's arm.

"What? You do. Every time you see Garrett, you practically drool all over yourself."

Jenna huffed. "I do not."

"Whatever." Sophie returned her gaze to Chloe.

"Oh, no." Chloe shook her head. "I'm not getting in the middle of that." She gestured toward the notepad on which Lori had written several names. "Who are the choices?"

"My money's on Greg Bozeman," Sophie said.

Chloe laughed again. "You've got to be joking." Greg was the biggest flirt in town, more so than even her younger brother, Owen.

"Think about it," Sophie said. "It would be the biggest feather in her cap so far."

Chloe shook her head. "I'll believe it when I see it. What are my other choices?"

"Daisy Ford," Lori said, naming one of the waitresses down at the Primrose Café. "Jesse Bradshaw, Andrew Canton." Lori read off a few other names before tossing in Bernie Shumaker, who had to be as old as Blue Falls.

"Okay, now I know you all have lost it."

Sophie shrugged. "Got to do something. It's a slow night."

They all froze.

"You did *not* just say that," Lori said.

They all looked toward the emergency entrance as if Sophie's words would tempt a herd of sick and injured to start flooding the ER. When the doors remained free of patients, they breathed a collective sigh of relief.

"What about you, Chloe?" Jenna asked, grinning. "You're single. Maybe we should put your name on the list."

Chloe lifted her package of cupcakes. "On that note, my new best friends and I are headed to the break room."

She'd just sat down and ripped away the plastic wrapping when she heard the siren. Considering one of the hospital's two ambulances sat outside the ER, this one had to be coming from the rodeo. Leaving her snack behind, she hurried back to the ER just as the paramedics were unloading their patient.

"What have we got?" she asked Dale Marsh, one of the paramedics.

"Male, thirty-one, name Wyatt Kelley. Took a bull horn to the side and the lower abdomen."

As she got her first look at the cowboy, she noticed his shirt soaked with blood. "Put him in trauma one."

Chloe started directing the nurses to remove both the cowboy's protective vest and his shirt so she could assess the seriousness of the guy's injuries. He'd been out cold when they wheeled him in, but when they lifted him he moaned in agony. As they laid him back, his eyes shot wide open and locked on her.

"Are you trying to kill me?" he asked, his voice breathless and strained.

She smiled, hoping to calm him. "Quite the opposite, handsome. You'll be good as new before you know it." A lot of doctors she'd worked with remained detached and clinical when working with patients, but that wasn't her style. She'd tried, and just couldn't stick to it. Wanting to help people and caring about them were the reasons she'd become a doctor in the first place. Maybe she'd burn out sooner, but she'd deal with that when the time came.

Chloe squeezed his hand then got back to work flushing his wounds. She pulled out a sliver of horn that had broken off and directed the nurses to start antibiotics so the bacteria from the horn didn't do the guy in. When she was able to see the wounds better, a deep laceration just below where his safety vest had ended and a puncture wound in his left side, she knew he needed surgery.

She made eye contact with Jenna. "Get Dr. Pierce in here."

Jenna nodded and hurried out of the trauma area.

"Please tell me Dr. Pierce isn't in charge of the morgue," the cowboy said.

Despite the pain he was in, the guy still managed to hang on to his sense of humor. She was pretty sure she'd be howling in agony.

"Not for this little scratch, cowboy."

"Wyatt."

She nodded. "Nice to meet you, Wyatt. I'm Dr. Brody."

He gritted his teeth against a wave of pain. "Gotta say, you're way prettier than most of the ER docs I've seen."

She shook her head. "See, you're not hurt too badly if you can flirt." The reality was his injuries weren't minor, but she didn't need him freaking out about how he wasn't going to be sitting on a bull anytime in the near future. These guys lived pretty spare unless they were in the big money, and Blue Falls hadn't quite made it to the big-time rodeo circuit yet.

"Hon, there's always time to flirt until you stop breathing." As if to contradict himself, he caught his breath as his injuries sent another jolt of pain through his body.

The good thing about Blue Falls being so small, it didn't take Dr. Pierce, the surgeon, long to reach the hospital.

Chloe took Wyatt's hand. "We're going to send you to surgery now and get you fixed up. Dr. Pierce will take good care of you." She gestured toward where the surgeon was walking by on his way to prep for surgery.

"He's not as pretty as you," Wyatt said, drawing a chuckle from Chloe.

When she started to step away, Wyatt squeezed her hand with a surprising grip considering the shape he was in. When her eyes met his, her heart skipped a beat. Damn, he was good-looking, even dirt- and blood-covered and with his face pale from the pain and blood loss. An unexpected heat rushed through her before she grabbed on to some professionalism and gave his hand a quick squeeze before releasing it.

"See you on the other side, cowboy."

Wyatt gave her a crooked grin. "Promise?"

She just smiled and sent him off to surgery.

"Yep, we definitely need to add you to the pool list," Lori said. "In fact, I think you just jumped to the top of it."

"Wyatt and Chloe sitting in a tree," Sophie said in a singsong voice. "K-i-s-s-i-n-g."

Chloe made as if she were going to throw one of her used surgical gloves at Sophie, sending the nurse scurrying away with a laugh. "Hard to pair me with someone who doesn't live here."

"India's and Skyler's husbands didn't live here, either, when they met them," Sophie called back.

Jenna deposited her used gloves in the hazardous waste bin. "And they just happened to be hot cowboys, too."

Chloe rolled her eyes and disposed of her own gloves. After thoroughly washing her hands and arms, she left the ER with a wave to the nurses. "I'm going to go finish my date with a cupcake."

"Save one for that delicious cowboy," Sophie called down the corridor.

She wasn't sure if it was the nurses' teasing, Wyatt Kelley's flirting, or the way her heart had stuttered when he'd held her hand and met her eyes, but she kept thinking about him throughout the rest of her shift. The cupcakes didn't distract her. Neither did dealing with a toddler who'd eaten an electric-lime crayon. When she tried to focus on anything else, her mind kept sliding back to the rugged angle of Wyatt's square jaw and those blue-gray eyes that had watched her with more interest than anyone with his abdomen ripped open should have been able to muster.

Even after her shift was over, she hung around. She figured the nurses would have a field day with that, but she didn't care. She kept telling herself it was professional interest, that she wanted to make sure her patient made it through surgery. She was so wrapped up in trying to convince herself she wasn't interested in Wyatt Kelley for anything other than medical reasons that she nearly ran into Dr. Pierce as he came out of the short corridor that led to surgery.

"You're still here?" His forehead wrinkled as he glanced at the clock on the wall.

"Yeah. Just checking on a few things before I leave." She nodded toward the surgical area. "How's Mr. Kelley?"

"In one piece, though he's not going to be riding in the foreseeable future. Maybe ever."

She didn't know Wyatt, but her heart hurt for him at that bit of news. She'd been around enough cowboys in her life to know they didn't like having to face hanging it up.

Several long moments after Dr. Pierce left, Chloe continued to stare down the corridor toward the double doors that led to surgery. She'd spent mere minutes with Wyatt, but she didn't like the image that formed in her mind of the light going out of his beautiful eyes as his future was ripped away. Why she cared so much, she had no idea. But she did.

Chapter Two

Wyatt started to wake when he heard voices. He couldn't distinguish actual words through the fog in his head, but the conversation nearby was enough to pull him toward the surface. As he listened, he could gradually make out words from the murmuring voices. *Surgery. Out. Night.* It was like listening to a radio station that was mostly static with only the occasional intelligible word.

He knew there was something he could do to help make sense of what was going on, but damned if he could remember what it was. So he lay still and listened to the voices—two women—and searched his brain for the answer. Then it hit him. He could open his eyes. But when he tried, that simple act proved to be easier thought than done.

What in the world had happened to him to make his body refuse to cooperate with his brain's commands?

"Dr. Pierce said the surgery went well last night," one of the voices said. There was something familiar about it, something that made him desperate to open his eyes. "I'm working at the clinic this afternoon, but let me know if anything changes."

She was leaving. No, she couldn't leave, not without him seeing the face that went with that voice. He concentrated on that one thought, the absolute necessity of opening his eyes before it was too late. At first, his eyelids did no more than flutter, but he concentrated harder and they finally lifted. The world around him came into focus bit by bit until his gaze fixed on her, the owner of the voice, the doctor who had joked with him in the ER.

"Will do," the nurse said.

Another nurse stuck her head in through the doorway. "I need help with Mrs. Walker in 221."

He watched as both nurses left the room without noticing he was awake. The doctor scanned what must be his medical chart. More of the fuzzy feeling in his head receded as he watched her make a notation on the chart then push her chin-length, reddish-brown hair behind her ear. He'd been in a lot of pain when he'd awakened in the ER, but he hadn't been so far gone that he didn't notice she was pretty. And now, as he fought his way out of what had to be a medicine-induced haze, he thought her even more so.

The doctor—what was her name? She'd told him, but he couldn't pull that information from his memory. Maybe he'd sustained another concussion in addition to the nasty lacerations. As she placed the chart at the end of his bed and turned to head for the door, he tried to say something but found his throat was as dry as cardboard. Instead of words, what came out was a strangled squawk. Yeah, that would get the ladies every time.

But it was enough to cause the doctor to lift her eyes to his.

"Well, hello there, sleepyhead," she said. She smiled as she moved to his side. "Sounds like you could use a drink." She poured him a cup of water from the pitcher on the bedside table then handed it to him.

When he reached for the cup, a sharp pain in his side caused him to suck in a breath then grit his teeth.

The doctor guided his hand to the cup and continued to steady it until she was sure he could hold it on his own.

"You'll want to not make any sudden moves for a while," she said. "No stretching, no lifting. If you need something, use the call button and a nurse will come help you."

He nodded though he hated the idea of being dependent. Maybe she was just being overly cautious. After all, this wasn't his first trip to the hospital, not even his first surgery. Chances were he'd be up and about in a few days. He might have to skip two or three rodeos, a hit on his finances he sure didn't need, but some things couldn't be helped. But if taking it easy in the hospital for a day or two helped him heal faster, then that's what he'd do. After all, he had a pretty doctor to tend his wounds.

The doctor reached to push the button to raise the head of the bed. That's when he noticed the name tag attached to her white lab coat. Dr. C. Brody. When the bed came to a stop, he brought the cup to his dry lips and took a drink. The water wasn't exactly cold as he liked it, but nothing had ever tasted so good. He started to down the rest of it when Dr. Brody stayed his hand.

"Go slowly."

Against his instinct, he did as she said and took another sip, letting it trickle down his throat as he met her eyes, pretty green ones with what looked like flecks of brown. When she broke eye contact and removed her hand from his, his gaze drifted to her lips. She wore a hint of pale pink lipstick, and something about the sight of it made his throat go dry again.

Dr. Brody crossed her arms. "So how are you feeling this morning?"

He glanced toward the window and saw that it was indeed daylight. "How long was I out?"

"Overnight and most of the morning. And you're feeling?" she asked again.

"Better than when I got here, but I bet that has a lot to do with whatever is in that." He pointed toward the IV pole that held two bags of liquids that were attached to his arm via tubes.

"Yeah, we kind of have to drug you up when you battle a bull and the bull wins."

He grinned at her. She was so unlike any doctor he'd ever met, funny and friendly. He pointed toward her name tag. "So what's the *C* for?"

"My first name."

He lifted a brow. "And that would be?"

"You know, I think I'll let you guess. That'll give you something to do while you recuperate."

"Caroline."

"Nope." With a self-satisfied smile, she turned to head toward the door again.

"Charlotte."

"No more guesses today," she called out as she slipped into the hallway and out of sight.

He might be less than twenty-four hours away from nearly getting his guts ripped out, but he found himself smiling. He liked a good challenge, and it seemed the lovely Dr. Brody was giving him exactly that.

CHLOE FINISHED HER hospital rounds several minutes later after listening to Henry Stillwater complain about everything from how the IV was hurting his hand to the inedible quality of the hospital food. She had to admit, the barely touched lunch on his table didn't look particularly appetizing. She wasn't even sure what the glob of yellowish orange goo was supposed to be.

As soon as she made her escape from Henry's room, her gaze shifted across the nurses' station to the first room she'd visited on her rounds. Wyatt's room. She tried telling herself that she was simply glad to see him awake and on the mend, but she could still feel the buzz in her middle that had started the moment she'd looked at him to find him watching her. The buzz that had only increased when she'd helped him grip the cup of water. A strange giddiness had blossomed to life within her when he'd tried to guess her name and she'd decided to keep him guessing.

While she was friendly and often teased her patients in the hope of taking their minds off their pain, her few minutes with Wyatt had felt different. And that wasn't wise because as soon as he was discharged he'd go home, a home that wasn't in Blue Falls. She didn't really know him and shouldn't care if he left as long as she'd done her job and set him on a path to recovery. But as soon as she'd exited his room, she'd started thinking about the next time she'd see him. Because she would see him once more, tomorrow when she was due to make hospital rounds again.

"You okay?"

Chloe jerked her attention away from Wyatt's doorway to where Sophie stood on the other side of the desk giving her a curious stare.

"Yeah, just remembered a call I have to make later this afternoon."

Sophie glanced over her shoulder, straight toward Wyatt's doorway. "Uh-huh."

Ignoring the suspicion in Sophie's voice, Chloe made a show of pulling her phone from her pocket and checking it. "Well, I have appointments at the clinic beginning in ten minutes." She nodded toward Henry's room. "You might want to get Henry something sweet from the vending machine. It'll probably make the rest of your shift more pleasant."

Sophie nodded. After all, it wasn't the first time they'd dealt with Henry's crankiness. "Good idea."

Chloe made her escape before Sophie could shift her focus back to Wyatt again. Though the left-hand corridor was closer to the exit next to the clinic, it also led past Wyatt's door. So Chloe made an unnecessary stop by the restroom located down the right-side corridor to give herself an excuse for going that direction. She wasn't normally a coward, but she'd never been crazy attracted to a patient before, either.

Once inside the restroom, she crossed to the sink and stared at herself in the mirror. Was that heightened color in her cheeks? She shook her head as she turned on the cold water and splashed some onto her face. She had to set aside the attraction before she saw him again. The last thing she needed was to blush like this in front of Wyatt. She could be cool and professional one more day, and then she was off work the following two days. Maybe Wyatt would be discharged by the time she had to walk these halls again.

Her afternoon was filled with so many appointments that she didn't have time to think about Wyatt or her attraction to the unlucky cowboy. But as she left the clinic at the end of the day, she had to fight the urge to go back to the hospital to check on him. Instead, she turned toward her car. When she was in the driver's seat, she didn't immediately start the engine. Though she was tired from a long day, part of her didn't want to go home, not when she was still feeling strange about a man she barely knew. The last thing she needed was her dad or either of her brothers sensing something was off about her and digging until they found out what it was.

She glanced at herself in the rearview mirror. "Stop being an idiot."

Even though she told herself to stop thinking about Wyatt, her thoughts kept going back to that grin of his, the one he shot in her direction despite the pain he was experiencing. She'd seen his type before, tough as thick leather and used to charming the pants right off a gal. Well, she wasn't a buckle bunny happy to draw a cowboy's attention. If she wanted a cowboy, she didn't have to wait for one to stroll into town, or be wheeled into her ER. This was Texas, after all. Cowboys were a dime a dozen, even without the regular rodeos bringing them to Blue Falls.

It was a ten-mile drive out to her family's ranch, and she told herself that she could think about Wyatt and his grin until she pulled into the driveway. Then she needed to leave those memories behind. Her thoughts wandered back to how he'd flirted with her in the ER, the fine cut of his chest and abdomen that she'd noticed despite his injuries, the way his eyes crinkled at the edges when he smiled. Though she'd never seen him standing, she imagined he was one of those guys who had a sexy saunter, the kind that made women think losing their pants might not be such a bad idea.

The moment the entrance to the ranch came into

view, she forced thoughts of Wyatt Kelley from her mind, replacing them with anything she could think of—the acreage of the ranch, the book she was reading, trying to remember the names of all the women her brother Owen had dated. That last one took long enough that she was parking next to the house by the time she ran out of names.

Once inside, she changed into a pair of jeans and a T-shirt, then mixed up a batch of cornbread muffins to go with the roast she'd put in the Crock-Pot that morning. The delicious smells filling the kitchen reminded her of Henry's complaints about his hospital food, which of course led her to wondering if Wyatt hated it, too. Or was he so used to eating junk on the road that hospital meals were actually a step up?

Damn it, here she was thinking about him again.

The back door opening caused her to jump, but thankfully her dad and brothers didn't notice as they hung their hats on the rack by the door and slipped off their dirty boots.

"That sure smells good," her dad said as he crossed to the refrigerator and pulled out a cold root beer, his favorite drink. He downed about half the bottle in one go, following it with a satisfied smack of his lips. "How was your day?"

"Fine, long. Henry Stillwater's in the hospital again."

Garrett, her older brother, walked to the kitchen island and nabbed a couple of the white chocolate-covered pretzels she'd been snacking on. "That old coot is in the hospital so much, I'm beginning to think he has a crush on you."

Chloe snorted. "More like he should stop smoking, but I'd be less surprised if UT decided to get rid of their football team."

Owen, her younger brother, snatched the pretzel bag from Garrett. "So, did that bull rider survive last night?"

A momentary flare of panic hit her right in the chest, fear that he'd somehow found out about her attraction to Wyatt. But unless Owen had suddenly developed the ability to read minds, there was no way he could know. Unless one of the nurses made some comment about her flirting in the ER.

"Yeah. Dr. Pierce had to sew him up, but he'll make it."

"Huh. I thought he might be a goner after what that bull did to him."

Chloe didn't want to encourage her brother to share any gory details so she turned to the Crock-Pot and started dishing up bowls of roast.

While her family ate dinner, as they had countless times before, Chloe found it hard to pay attention to what her dad and brothers were saying. She kept thinking about how close Wyatt had come to dying. She might not know him beyond a few minutes of conversation, but the idea that his life might have been snuffed out the night before bothered her. Really bothered her.

Of course it did. She was a doctor, charged with saving lives.

Even the lives of ridiculously good-looking cowboys.

"Earth to Chloe," Owen said as he waved a hand in front of her face.

"What? Sorry."

"How are things in la-la land?"

She swatted his hand away. "I'm just tired. Didn't sleep well last night."

Normally, sleeping like a log wasn't a problem, especially on days when she worked a twelve-hour shift. But for some reason, she'd woken up several times the night before. She'd gotten the sense she'd been dreaming a lot, but she couldn't remember about what. Now she wondered if it might have been about a certain injured bull rider.

"I think I'm going to turn in early if someone else can handle the dishes."

"Go on," Garrett said. "I'll get them."

She gave him a tired smile. "Thanks."

"Good, because I got a hot date," Owen said as he scooted away from the table.

"You always have a hot date," Garrett said.

"You should try it sometime, big brother."

Not really in the mood to talk about her brothers' dating lives or lack thereof, Chloe headed to the bathroom. After a quick shower to wash away the day, she trudged into her bedroom and climbed into bed. But despite the fact that she really was tired, sleep seemed far away as she stared out the window at the sliver of moon.

The tug of loneliness made a reappearance, as it had several times recently. It didn't make much sense considering she was around people all day long and still lived at home with her family. When she'd first started feeling as if something was missing a couple of weeks earlier, she'd wondered if for some reason she'd started missing her mother again. Honestly, she missed her mom every day if she thought about it, despite the fact it'd been more than twenty years since her death.

But as she thought about that loss now, it didn't seem

to match the empty spot that had opened up inside Chloe. Not knowing how to tackle the unfamiliar and unwanted feeling proved frustrating. She was the type of person who saw a problem or obstacle and faced it head-on. But how did you do that if you couldn't identify the culprit?

She listened to the movements of her dad and brother downstairs, and it hit her that they were every bit as alone as she was. Only Owen had an active love life, but even he showed no signs of getting serious with anyone.

Chloe laid the back of her hand against her forehead and searched for the moment when she'd first noticed the emptiness. She realized after several minutes that it had been shortly after her friend Linnea had announced her engagement and started planning her dream wedding. Is that what Chloe wanted—the big wedding, the happily ever after?

Of course she did. So did most women. But it had always been a "someday" sort of thing. It seemed as if someday were catching up with her, but getting married and having a family of her own wasn't as simple as it sounded, either. You couldn't just go shopping for a husband like you could a new car. Not to mention that her schedule was always crazy busy between working at the clinic and hospital and helping out her family.

Still, she couldn't dispel that line of thought as she tried to force herself to go to sleep. Her mind began to manufacture scenes as she started to drift, scenes of her with her own house, a big yard where two small children laughed and played. She looked toward a barn in the distance, saw someone walk out of it and head toward her. Her heart leaped and the excitement of anticipation rushed through her. As the man drew closer, the thought that he was her husband, the love of her life, settled comfortably within her.

When he came near enough for her to see his face, she smiled. Wyatt didn't stop until he pulled her into his arms and kissed her with so much passion that she knew in the deepest part of her heart that she was the luckiest woman in the world.

Chapter Three

Wyatt flipped through the channels on the TV for what had to be the tenth time. Still nothing remotely interesting. He was beginning to look forward to a nurse coming to check his vitals just so he'd have something to do.

As if the cosmos had heard his plea, someone walked into his room. Fate had taken pity on him because it was pretty Dr. Brody. She glanced at the TV, where he'd paused on some sort of infomercial for jewelry cleaner, and smiled.

"Got a lot of silver you need to clean?"

He flicked off the TV. "Daytime TV is garbage."

"Yeah, sorry we don't have any decent movie channels."

"Is it possible to die of boredom?"

She lifted his chart from the end of the bed. "Afraid not, though I'm sure it feels that way." She made a couple of notations on the chart before returning it to its previous spot.

"So, I think I've figured out your name."

"That so?" Dr. Brody walked around to the side of his bed and checked the fluids in his IV bags.

"Yeah. You look like a Carly."

"Swing and a miss."

"Christa."

"Nope."

When he started to guess again, she shook her head. "Only two guesses a day."

He lifted a brow. "Just how long do you think I'm going to be in here?"

"That's partly up to Dr. Pierce." She pointed toward the IV bags. "But we'll start gradually lowering the dosage on these as well as the painkiller."

"So what do I get when I guess your name?"

A hint of a smile tugged at the edge of her mouth. "The satisfaction of a mystery solved."

He laughed a little, and damn if it didn't hurt his middle. "You must have gone to the medical school where they teach doctors to have an actual personality."

"Oh, this is all me, there way before med school."

"Naturally quick with comebacks, huh?"

"That's what happens when you grow up with brothers. Couldn't beat them up, couldn't outrun them, but I could win in a smart-mouth contest any day."

She shifted as if leaving already, and he caught himself just before he reached out and grabbed her arm. "Seriously, when can I get out of this place?"

Her light demeanor fell away. "You sustained significant injuries. If that horn had cut a little deeper, you might not be talking to me right now. You'd at the very best be feeling a lot worse. So you need to give your body time to repair itself."

"That's not a definite answer."

"Because I don't know a definite answer. It depends on how quickly and how well your injuries begin to heal."

Frustration welled up within him. He was not good

at lying around doing nothing, especially when he was pretty sure he'd exhausted his limited health-care coverage by the time he rolled out of surgery.

"Is there anyone we can call to let them know you're here?" she asked. "Having visitors would make the days go by more quickly."

He shook his head. Even if he were back in Wyoming, there wasn't anyone close enough that he'd be able to call them up and have them sit in a hospital with him.

"Tell you what. I'm done with my rounds in a few minutes. I'll bring you some magazines, maybe a crossword puzzle book. That will help pass the time until something decent comes on TV tonight."

"Any chance I can at least go sit outside?"

He had to give her credit. She looked genuinely sorry when she shook her head. "Not yet."

He was going to go stark-raving mad.

"I know it stinks. But I'll be back with some issues of *Woman's Day* before you know it."

"You are evil," he said, at least thankful that she was personable and he had her brief visits to look forward to.

"Who, me? I'm an angel." She pretended to buff an invisible halo before laughing a little and heading for the door. "Hang in there, cowboy."

She knew his name, but there was something about the way she called him "cowboy" that he liked. Still, part of him enjoyed imagining her saying his name right before he kissed those pink lips. Yeah, he'd been daydreaming about his doctor. That's what happened when you were full of stitches, unable to get out of bed and had way too many hours of staring at the wall. Not to mention not having been on a date in a while.

Wyatt was pretty sure the minutes slowed after she left. He stared out the narrow window, but the view of the empty helipad lost his interest pretty quickly. He closed his eyes and tried to think of every possible female name that started with a *C*. He wanted to know the doc's name, but he sure didn't want to stay in the hospital long enough to guess it. Maybe he'd get lucky tomorrow. He settled on the two most likely choices then was left with nothing to do again. He finally resorted to turning on the TV and found an older-than-dirt action movie. It wasn't a great film, but it was better than resorting to counting the divots in the ceiling tiles.

He was beginning to wonder how the movie even got made when Dr. Brody returned, the promised magazines in hand. He muted the TV as she placed the magazines on the rolling table and pushed it close so he could reach it.

"I behaved," she said as he sifted through the stack of magazines. One about hunting and fishing, another about cars, *Sports Illustrated* and… "Mostly."

He laughed at the copy of *Cosmopolitan*. "Maybe it'll help me figure out how women's minds work."

"You mean you don't think you know that already?"

"There's not a man alive who's figured that out."

"Maybe you all just aren't observant enough."

Wyatt shook his head, not going down that road filled with land mines. "Thanks for the magazines."

She reached into her coat pocket, pulled out a candy bar and set it beside the magazines and the crossword puzzle book. "Figured this might come in handy, too."

"You were in my head."

"No, I just see what passes for dessert here."

Thunder rumbled outside, drawing their attention to the window. It had grown dark out, even though it was still a few hours from nightfall. Wyatt noticed that a weather broadcast had broken in on the movie. The radar image was several shades of red with lots of indications of lightning strikes.

"That doesn't look good," he said.

Dr. Brody sighed. "Just in time for my drive home."

"Guess you'll have to stay here until it passes." When she glanced at him, he winked at her.

"If I didn't know better, I'd swear you ordered the storm."

"If I had that much power, I'd heal myself so I could get out of this awful bed. My back feels like I fell off a building."

"Here, let's see if we can do something about that." She crossed to the other side of the room, where an empty bed sat awaiting another unfortunate hospital guest. She grabbed a pillow and stepped close to his side. "Carefully lean forward."

He bit his lip to keep from wincing, but then his breath caught for a different reason. Dr. Brody grasped his shoulder as she tucked the pillow so that it stretched from his lower back to his shoulders. She stood close enough that he could smell her feminine scent, something flowery but not overwhelming.

"You smell nice."

She stopped moving for a moment, and he thought he heard her breath catch, too. But when she eased him back against the pillow and took a step away, she smiled.

"Well, you're used to smelling antiseptic and bleach," she said, deflecting his compliment.

A loud crash of thunder that sounded as if it were right above his room caused her to jump. Right on the heels of the thunder, the sky opened up and released a deluge of rain. In the space of a couple of seconds, the helipad became obscured.

"Even Mother Nature thinks you should stay and keep me company," he said.

"Since I didn't bring my canoe to work, I think you're right."

He was actually sort of surprised when the doc pulled up a chair and propped her feet on the end of his bed.

"So, Wyatt Kelley, tell me something about yourself."

"Not much to tell."

"Everyone has a story."

"And some of them aren't all that interesting. What about you?"

"What do you want to know?"

"Your name."

She smiled, and he spotted a mischievous glint in her eyes. "Nice try."

"Okay, are you originally from Blue Falls?"

"Yep, born and raised on a ranch outside of town. My turn. Where are you from?"

"Laramie, Wyoming."

"Long way from home."

He shrugged, irked that even that slight motion sent a twinge through his injured side. "Not really. I mainly live on the road."

"Traveling from rodeo to rodeo."

He nodded.

"I don't know how you guys do that, especially climbing onto bulls. My younger brother did rodeo for a while, but he was a roper. At least he wasn't cheating death every time he got in the chute."

"Most of the time I don't even think about it."

"Seriously?"

"Yeah. I've been around rodeo all my life. It's nothing out of the ordinary."

Dr. Brody shook her head slowly. "Maybe all of you have just had one too many concussions to know better."

"Maybe, but the crowds love it. We crazy bull riders help to bring people in to events like your town's rodeos."

"Yeah, but I end up patching you guys up. Do you all have contests to see who can get the most broken bones or stitches in a year?"

"No, but maybe I should start that bet. I'd have a good chance of winning."

She snorted a little laugh that told him just what she thought of that idea.

Another loud boom of thunder set off a car alarm outside, and in the next moment the electricity went out. Dr. Brody immediately jumped to her feet and headed for the door, but before she got there the backup generators kicked in.

"Be back in a bit," she said then disappeared.

He listened to the flurry of footsteps out in the hall, as the staff checked on patients to make sure all the necessary monitors and equipment were operating correctly. Wyatt glanced at the TV and realized the angriest part of the storm sat right smack on top of Blue Falls. After a storm like this, there would no doubt be necessary cleanup. If only he weren't a prisoner of his injuries, maybe he could pick up a couple days of work. Lord knew his wallet could always use the extra cash.

That thought took him back to Dr. Brody's comments about how he put his life in danger every time he settled himself atop a bull. But it was all he knew beyond basic manual labor. Maybe he could have done something else if he'd applied himself, but rodeo had gotten into his blood early and he'd not thought much beyond it. Good damn thing that bull two nights ago hadn't done anything that was irreparable.

But what if it had? He'd be totally screwed.

Maybe he needed to think about a plan for when his rodeo days were over. Even the best of the best had to quit riding sometime. If he started chatting up some of his contacts now, maybe he could plant the seed that would grow into some sort of rodeo-related job after he quit riding. Maybe he'd even follow in his grandfather's footsteps and become an announcer.

But that was down the road. All he needed to do now was heal enough to escape this damn bed and get back on the road. He was losing precious time, points and money, none of which he could afford.

Dr. Brody stayed gone so long that he'd begun to think maybe she'd headed home. He hoped not, and not just because he liked her company. The storm hadn't slackened much. Even he would have pulled over in this mess and let it pass. He might ride bulls for a living, but that wasn't as dangerous as driving when you couldn't see the road in front of you.

Using the dim light above his bed, he started flipping through the fishing-and-hunting magazine. He honestly wasn't much for hunting, but he liked the solitude and quiet of a morning of fishing. He had a lot of fond memories of fly-fishing with his grandfather on the Laramie and North Platte Rivers, outings he often wished he could relive just once.

Not wanting to travel down memory lane, he tossed the magazine back onto the table and looked at the TV screen. It appeared the storm was moving quickly. As if to confirm that observation, the rain subsided outside. He shifted his focus to the doorway and watched as people walked back and forth, but none of them were the person he wanted to see. He'd barely had that thought when she popped her head in the door.

"I'm going to see if I can float home now. Behave yourself." She gestured toward the magazines. "And good luck figuring out the mysteries of the female mind."

He snorted. "I'll settle for figuring out your name. I'm confident I'll get it right tomorrow. I've got two good guesses ready to go."

"You'll have to hang on to them. I'm off for the next couple of days."

Wyatt's heart sank. The days were long and boring enough without her brief visits. What the devil was he going to look forward to without them?

"Then I get six guesses when you come back."

She smiled. "You'll need them."

Wyatt tried to occupy himself with some more channel surfing and reading the magazines. He even pulled out the crossword-puzzle book and worked a few. But his mind wandered and he started writing down all the *C* names he could think of down the margin of one of the puzzles.

When a nurse came in after the shift change that

evening, he chatted her up a little before springing the question uppermost in his mind. "Hey, could you tell me what Dr. Brody's first name is?"

"Sure," she said with a smile that made her eyes twinkle. "It's Chloe." The nurse lowered her voice. "Don't tell the other docs, but she's our favorite."

His, too.

He waited until the nurse, Sophie, left the room before he let his mind fix on the lovely doctor's name. Chloe. It fit her. But with his curiosity satisfied, there was no way he was going to give her the correct answer. For however long he was stuck here, he needed something to look forward to. And if "guessing" the wrong names kept Chloe coming back, he'd toss every crazy name he could at her.

He smiled and felt better than he had since she'd left.

AFTER WORKING A bit more at the clinic, Chloe raced to her car through the still falling rain. Once inside, she wiped the water from her face and smoothed back her wet hair. She stared at the rivulets streaming down the windshield. She'd done it. When she'd awakened from the dream about Wyatt being her husband and kissing her as if it were the end of time, she'd doubted she'd be able to face him without blushing so brightly she'd be mistaken for a solar flare.

She'd considered avoiding him and asking Dr. Pierce to check on him instead. It wouldn't be unusual for the surgeon to do a post-op visit. She'd even been on the verge of calling Dr. Pierce before she'd caught herself, chastised herself for being so silly. She rarely turned away from a challenge or obstacle, so she wasn't about to let an admittedly very nice dream about a sexy cowboy send her running.

Though she'd been antsy when she arrived at his room, the feeling had quickly faded when she'd found him looking more bored than she could recall ever seeing anyone. She'd nearly laughed and felt sorry for him at the same time. During her one hospitalization for pneumonia, when she'd been thirteen, she'd been bored out of her mind, too, and she'd had family and friends visiting her and keeping her company.

Wyatt was a thousand miles from home, stuck in a town where he knew no one, unable to even get out of bed. That had to suck for a guy like him, always on the go. He was the poster child for someone who could use a friend right now. And it wasn't the first time she'd spent extra time with a patient she felt needed it. The other doctors called her a softie. Chloe had decided long ago she could live with that label. To her, it was way better than becoming so detached that patients became a list of symptoms on case files instead of people with hopes and fears and who would rather be anywhere than in a hospital bed.

She started the car and headed home through the rain that was letting up even more. Her thoughts drifted back to when she was a child, when she would hang out at the hospital while her mom was at work there. Her mother had been a nursing assistant, but she'd been great with the patients, calming them, making them laugh, gifting them with a smiling face and a sympathetic ear.

Chloe's memories settled on Beatrice Collins, a tiny slip of an old woman who'd been in the hospital back when Chloe had been about eight years old. Even though it'd been more than two decades since then, Chloe could still remember how very alone Beatrice had looked in her bed. The sad part was that she'd had family. They simply hadn't come to see her. Chloe's mom had done what she could to cheer up the older woman, but Beatrice had still died alone in the hospital. Chloe remembered her mother being upset about it, not so much that Beatrice had died but that she'd been so lonely in her final days. Chloe could still hear her mother saying, "I think she died of a broken heart as much as anything."

She hadn't thought of Beatrice in a long time, but the image wouldn't leave her. Wyatt was out of the woods now and otherwise young and healthy even if he did wear the scars of his trade. Even so, she found herself pulling into a parking space in front of the Primrose Café. Before she could talk herself into driving on home like any sensible person, she got out of her car, walked inside and proceeded to order two meals to go. While she waited, she texted Garrett to let him know the Brody men were on their own tonight without telling them why.

By the time her order was ready, the rain had moved out. A sliver of the sun setting in the west had found a crack in the clouds and spread out its rays as if comforting the landscape after the storm. She took a deep breath of the rain-scented air before slipping back into her car and retracing the route to the hospital.

Luckily, the staff seemed to be busy elsewhere as she made her way down the hallway and into Wyatt's room. "Did you miss me?"

He looked up from where he was reading the *Sports*

Illustrated and scrunched his forehead in concentration. "Who are you again?"

She lifted an eyebrow at him. "Just for that, I'm taking this chicken-fried steak to someone who will appreciate it." She spun toward the door.

"Wait. Don't tease a guy like that."

Chloe turned halfway toward him and lifted one of the takeout containers. "So you do want this?"

"I don't care if you have a gas-station hot dog in there. It's got to be better than the food here."

She honestly felt sorry for the cafeteria workers. They no doubt worked hard and got no love. Still, facts were facts. Hospital food was, as a general rule, dreadful.

Chloe placed both meals on the rolling table, which Wyatt had positioned in front of him. "Scoot." She motioned for him to move his legs so she could sit on the edge of his bed.

Wyatt opened his container and inhaled deeply. "Will you marry me?"

Chloe froze for a moment before forcing herself to laugh. She hoped he didn't notice the jolt that went through her at his joking proposal. What was it with Wyatt and all these references to marriage? She seriously needed to get a grip. Just because she'd decided maybe it was time to start her own family before she was too old did not mean she had to latch on to the first guy who crossed her path. Sure, he was good-looking—really good-looking—but you couldn't base a relationship on looks alone, even if that person didn't live his life on the road cheating death most of the year.

Remembering that she hadn't made any sort of response to his "proposal," Chloe shook her head and opened her plastic utensils. "I think you might have that concussion after all."

Thankfully, he didn't pursue the topic, instead diving into his meal as if he hadn't eaten in days. Maybe he hadn't had a decent dinner in a long time. She'd been around enough rodeo cowboys, especially the ones who weren't at the top of the rankings, to know they didn't have enough cash to toss toward pricey food.

"So, what's life like in Wyoming? I've never been there."

He shrugged, and she saw the wince that motion caused.

"Probably not much different than here, just a lot colder in the winter."

"How'd you get into bull riding?"

"Looked like fun."

Chloe stopped eating and stared at him. "You're going to make me work hard for every scrap of information, aren't you?"

He met her gaze. "Frustrating, isn't it?"

She knew he was talking about her first name. "Fair point."

He took another bite of his gravy-covered chicken-fried steak and chased it with a drink of tea. She'd just taken a bite of her green beans when he spoke again.

"My grandpa was a rodeo announcer, so I was around rodeo from the time I was young. Can't really say why I chose bull riding other than I was full of myself, thought I could do anything."

"How long have you been riding? I can tell you've had several broken bones and probably more cuts and bruises than you can count."

"Since I was thirteen in junior rodeo."

"I still can't believe they let kids ride bulls."

"They're not the rank ones you see in rodeos like the other night."

"They're still bulls with horns that can do damage."

"Have to learn sometime. Is it any different than being a doctor? When did you know that's what you wanted to do?"

She stared at him then sighed. "You need to stop making valid points."

He laughed and winced again.

"Are your injuries causing you pain? We can look at the dosage of the painkillers again."

Wyatt shook his head. "No, nothing I can't handle. I want off those drugs as soon as possible." The intensity of his words caused her to look at him more closely. Had he experienced a problem with painkillers in the past?

They ate in silence for a couple of minutes before she noticed Wyatt was watching her.

"What?"

"I was wondering why you decided to come back."

This time, she was the one to shrug. "I've worked here long enough to know how incredibly long and boring the days can be when you're stuck in the hospital. It's as if time moves slower inside these walls."

"That's perceptive."

She smiled then wiped the edge of her mouth with her napkin. "I like to think I'm a bit smarter than the average bear."

"Guess you'd have to be to become a doctor."

"It's certainly not easy. There were times when I didn't think I could cram one more medical fact in my head or it would explode or start oozing out my ears."

"Nice image."

She gave a little bow. "Thank you, thank you very much."

"You make a habit of this, then?"

"I've been known to spend extra time with patients, watch a movie or two, hand out cupcakes from time to time. I'm probably too softhearted."

"No, it's great. More doctors should be that way."

"There are lots of doctors who care or they wouldn't be doing what they're doing, especially in small communities like this."

"But do they bring their patients dinner or sit and watch TV with them?"

"Well, no, but I understand the need for distance, especially if you want a long career. Lots of people we see don't make it, and it carves a little part out of you if you've allowed yourself to get close to them."

"But you do it anyway."

Chloe twirled her fork in her mashed potatoes. "I can't seem to help it."

When Wyatt didn't say anything in response, she looked up to find him staring at her as if he'd just stumbled upon the eighth wonder of the world. He seemed to realize he was staring and shifted his gaze back to his food.

"I'm surprised a doctor would bring me fried food."

"You shouldn't eat it every day, but sometimes you just need comfort food. Like when I get sick, I'm going to eat some chicken and dumplings, carbs be damned."

When they both finished their meals, Chloe tossed the containers in the trash. She didn't resume her seat on the edge of the bed, but she picked up the crossword book and flipped through the pages. Wyatt had already completed a dozen of the puzzles.

"Don't look so surprised," he said.

"What?"

He pointed toward the book. "You looked surprised I'd done any of those."

"You just haven't had the book that long."

"And a rodeo cowboy should have a lot harder time with it?"

She set the book down on the table and crossed her arms. "That is not what I meant at all. For all I know, there are Mensa members who ride bucking horses and chess champions who do tie-down roping. I think lots of people have hidden talents."

"What's yours?" He appeared to be having a hard time hiding a mischievous grin.

"I'll have you know that I'm the family Scrabble champ and have been since I was twelve."

"Yeah? Maybe you should broaden your competition."

"Is that a challenge, Mr. Kelley?"

"Only if you're willing to accept it, Dr. Brody."

"Then I guess you'll have to do everything you're told so you can get better and we can have a Scrabble duel before you leave." She took a step back from the side of Wyatt's bed. "And speaking of leaving, I really am going home this time."

"If you're bored on your days off, you know where I'll be."

She couldn't help but smile. "I'll keep that in mind."

When she stepped out of the room, she nearly collided with Sophie, who was wearing a too-happy smile. "Dr. Brody."

Chloe did her best not to utter an "oh, crap" at how loaded those two words from Sophie's mouth were. She remembered their earlier conversation about the matchmaking pool and wondered if she'd just opened herself up to a full-on assault by Verona Charles and her determination to make sure everyone in Blue Falls got paired up to live happily ever after.

Perhaps the bigger danger was how much a part of Chloe liked that idea.

Chapter Four

Chloe paused in slicing potatoes when she heard a text ping her phone. She activated the touch screen to see it was from Linnea. When she opened the message, it was a photo of the back of Linnea's wedding gown. The confection of satin, lace and pearl buttons looked as if it were out of a fairy tale. But that was to be expected. Linnea owned one of the nicest bridal stores in Dallas, and she'd snagged herself a prince. Well, not literally a prince, but Michael Benson could certainly treat Linnea like a princess. He was a handsome financial executive who made a good deal of money, and had captured Linnea's heart in record time.

A sigh escaped Chloe as she stared at the dress. She was thrilled for her best friend, but she wondered if she'd ever find someone who made her feel the way Michael made Linnea feel.

Her thoughts drifted to Wyatt Kelley, probably because he seemed to be the only guy on her radar at the moment. Maybe if Wyatt were local, she'd consider seeing if their conversations would lead to something else. She was normally pretty grounded and sensible, but for some reason she had to keep reminding herself that Wyatt would be gone in a matter of days. Besides, there was nothing between them other than some teasing and a few minutes spent together here and there.

"You okay, sis?"

Chloe closed the message on her phone before looking over her shoulder at Garrett. "Yeah. Why?"

"Because you've been staring at your phone for over a minute."

Surely it hadn't been that long. Had it? "Linnea just sent a text about her wedding dress."

Garrett walked up to the kitchen sink, turned on the water and proceeded to wash his hands. "Hope she has unlimited texting the way she's sending you photos almost faster than you can open them."

"Well, that's a bit of an exaggeration."

"Maybe, but I guarantee you Michael isn't sending photos of his tux and shoes and whatever else to his best man."

She bumped his shoulder with her own. "Just because guys are simplistic creatures doesn't mean we have to be."

Garrett turned around and leaned back against the sink. "So you're telling me that when you get engaged, you're going to send Linnea fifty photos a day of every little detail?"

There it was, that crazy reference to her getting married again. "Who knows? Maybe I'll send them to you and Owen, too."

Garrett snorted then headed toward the front door. "Need anything from town?"

"Nah, I'm good." Well, except for the memory of Wyatt from her dream springing into her head.

When Garrett was gone, she went back to slicing potatoes. It was a good thing she had a couple of days off, ones where she could immerse herself in tasks around the ranch and let the strange pull toward Wyatt fade. Part of her felt bad that he'd likely be bored crazy without anyone to visit him, but it wasn't her responsibility to keep him entertained. She'd already done more for him outside her professional duties than any other doctor likely would.

Still, as she went through the day cleaning the house, doing laundry and putting fresh hay in the horses' stalls out in the barn, her thoughts kept straying back to Wyatt. She actually had to fight the urge to drive into town to see him. Visiting him on days she worked and was already at the clinic or hospital was one thing, but how could she explain visiting someone she barely knew on her day off? And if Sophie and the other nurses had their way, Chloe would be in the town Cupid's matchmaking crosshairs. And just because Verona had gotten it right before with people whose other halves were supposed to just be passing through Blue Falls didn't mean that would be the case with Chloe.

Once she put the potatoes in the oven, she went out to the front porch to feed Roscoe and Cletus, the family's two basset hounds. As soon as she stepped through the doorway with the scoop of food in hand, the dogs hopped up from where they were dozing at the edge of the porch and trotted over to their matching bowls, their long ears swaying.

"Hey, fellas," she said as she scratched first Roscoe between the ears then Cletus. She laughed when they ignored her, their minds focused on dinner. Letting them chomp away, she went to sit at the top of the porch steps.

She watched as a hawk soared high above the pasture beyond the barn. The sound of horse hooves drew her attention back to ground level. Owen and her dad rode toward the barn from the south, what they all referred to as the back of the ranch. They'd been out checking the fence line after hearing about another strike on a nearby ranch by pranksters who for some reason thought it was great fun to cut ranchers' barbed-wire fences, allowing their cattle to escape. What they either didn't realize, or didn't care about, was that their vandalism was dangerous. A cow could get hurt or, worse, someone might hit them with a car and be injured or killed.

When her dad and brother dismounted, Owen took the reins of both horses and led them toward the barn. Her dad turned toward the house.

"Find any breaks in the fencing?" she asked when he came close enough to hear her.

"For now, everything is fine. Until they catch these bastards, we're going to have to keep a close eye on the whole spread."

"I saw Simon Teague in town yesterday," she said, speaking of the local sheriff. "He said they had something similar happen up in Runnels County a few months ago. He's been talking with the sheriff up there, but they never caught the people."

Her father shook his head. "If they were stealing the cattle, it would almost make sense. But this is just pure meanness."

"Simon said they're doing all the extra patrols they can."

"But there's no way he can be everywhere at once, not with what few men he has at his disposal."

"Maybe they'll get lucky."

Her dad grunted as if he weren't holding out much hope for that. After a moment, he seemed to set aside worries of the fence cutters and looked at her. "Hear you've made a new friend in that bull rider laid up at the hospital."

Well, hell. She guessed it was too much to hope that word wouldn't get out about her spending extra time with Wyatt. She shrugged as if it were no big deal. "Sort of stinks for him to be stuck in a hospital bed with no family or friends to keep him company. Doesn't even have a roommate at the moment."

A sad little smile stretched her dad's mouth. "You're so like your mother, lending aid and comfort to anyone who needs it."

"It's my job."

"It's more than that, always has been since you were a little girl befriending every kid at school who didn't have friends." He paused for a moment. "I wish your mom could see what a good woman you've grown up to be."

Chloe pressed her lips together and blinked a couple of times against sudden tears. One would think that after all this time, talking about her mom wouldn't make her want to cry. But at times, it felt as if she'd just talked to her mom, been held in her arms, only the day before.

Perhaps sensing how close her emotions were to the surface, maybe even feeling choked up himself, her dad climbed the steps beside her, patting her on the shoulder as he passed by.

Roscoe padded over and flopped down beside her, resting his head on her leg as if he knew she needed some comfort. She ran her hand over his head and down his back. He looked up at her with those big brown eyes, and her heart went gooey soft with love. Roscoe might be a dog, but he and Cletus were a part of the family.

"I see your sad puppy eyes, you adorable rascal."

"I don't envy the man who ends up falling for you," Owen said as he sauntered toward her. "He'll never beat out ol' Roscoe here."

Chloe scratched between Roscoe's ears again. He enjoyed that more than anything. "What's not to love? He adores me, doesn't talk back, isn't demanding."

Owen leaned against the edge of the porch, and she could tell he wanted to say something else.

"What is it?"

"Thought you should know that scuttlebutt around town is that you're Verona Charles's next project."

She sighed and stared out toward the road. "That woman needs to find her own man and maybe she'd stop poking around in everyone else's love lives."

"You've got a love life?"

Chloe snarled at him. "Be careful. I'll sic Roscoe on you."

Owen laughed. "I'm shaking."

"Go on, Roscoe. Get him. Use his arm as a chew toy."

"I think you could wrap my arm in bacon and these two still wouldn't rouse themselves to attack."

As if to prove his point, Roscoe let out a doggy sigh and closed his eyes as if about to take a nap while using her leg as a pillow.

Chloe shook her head at the dog. "Well, I guess I have to look elsewhere for my knight in shining armor."

"From what I hear, you already have. Maybe silver spurs instead of shining armor."

Chloe narrowed her eyes at her little brother. "Owen Brody, if you know what's good for you, you'll stop believing town gossip."

Owen whistled. "Hit a nerve, did I?"

"Owen," she said, warning in her voice.

He held up his hands. "Okay, okay. I'm backing off."

Chloe continued to sit outside after her brother followed their father inside. If people were already pairing up her and Wyatt based on her just trying to be friendly, how long before Wyatt got wind of it? And when he did, how was she supposed to face him without letting it show that she didn't mind as much as she should?

WYATT WATCHED THE minutes tick by on the clock, wondering when Chloe would be by to do her hospital rounds. If the other riders could see him now, laid up like an invalid and with nothing to look forward to beyond a visit from a doctor, no doubt they'd think him pathetic. Even the single guys on the circuit had someone—a girlfriend, brother, sister, best friend...parents. Most of the time, his lack of family didn't bother him. It was just the way things were. He had friends, but they were out on the circuit somewhere, heading to the next event and another batch of points.

He heard Chloe's voice from somewhere nearby, and his pulse jumped. Chances were if he'd met her in any other situation, he wouldn't be so fixated on her. Yes, she was pretty, but it wasn't as if she were the first pretty woman he'd ever seen. She was more like a lifeline to sanity than anything else, one he'd been denied the past two days.

Forty-eight hours of mind-destroying boredom. He'd read every one of the magazines she'd brought him cover to cover, even the *Cosmopolitan*, a fact he would never admit to anyone. *That* was boredom. In the wee hours when he couldn't sleep anymore, he'd finished the last puzzle in the crossword book, and he'd only had to cheat a handful of times.

But if Chloe was just a way to keep from being bored, why did he get more excited to see her than anyone else who traipsed into his room? Sure, he talked to everyone from the nurses to the gal who mopped the floors. But Chloe, for some reason, was different. Maybe it was nothing more than hers was the first face he'd seen when he'd awakened in the emergency room.

He really needed to stop being so damn philosophical.

"So, I hear you've been contrary the past couple of days," Chloe said as she breezed into his room with a scolding expression on her face.

"I deny that accusation."

"So you haven't been pestering the nurses to let you get up and saunter around the hospital?"

"I thought doctors liked to get patients up and out of bed as soon as possible."

"As soon *as possible*. We'd prefer not to risk undoing the work we've done. Trust me, you don't want to reinjure yourself. I'm sure it hurt enough the first time around."

"Fine," he said, unable to hide his frustration. "Then the least you can do is to play that game of Scrabble with me." He gestured toward the board on the rolling table that belonged to the still-empty second bed, where he'd already played the word *wander* for twenty points.

"Where did that come from?"

"Your friend Sophie."

Chloe rolled her eyes. "Of course it did."

What was that about? "Am I missing something?"

She waved away his question and walked toward the Scrabble board. "Well, that seems appropriate."

"What does?"

She pointed toward the tiles. "*Wander*. Sort of describes your life, doesn't it?"

He knew she didn't mean anything negative by it, but for some reason he suddenly felt as if his life didn't have a lot of meaning. That was odd since he enjoyed what he did. Wasn't that all anyone could ask for from a career, to enjoy it?

Chloe didn't wait for an answer, but instead selected her tiles from the bag, quickly rearranged them then played her word. She rolled the table toward him so he could see.

He barked a laugh, one that hurt a little less than it had before. "Ornery?"

"I wonder why that word came to mind."

He looked up at her and was struck anew by how pretty she was with those bright eyes, soft-looking skin and a smile always at the ready even when she was being serious.

"Can you honestly tell me you wouldn't be doing the same thing if our roles were reversed? You don't strike me as a woman who does idle very well."

She pressed her lips together for a moment. "Who knew cowboys were such good judges of character?"

"Have to be able to peg a bull's attitude."

"You're comparing me to a bull?"

He thought he'd made a huge tactical error until the edge of her mouth twitched. "Bullheaded, maybe."

She feigned offense with a dramatic gasp. "Pot, meet kettle."

He laughed again, and so did she.

"Okay, we'll get you on your feet in a few minutes, see how it goes."

At that news, he threw back the covers before she could change her mind. "Better avert your eyes, Doc."

"Oh, honey, you're not going to flash anything I haven't seen here a million times."

He raised an eyebrow at that, tempted to prove her wrong. The idea of making her blush sounded like the most fun he'd had in days.

"Hospital gowns aren't the most modest of attire," she said. "We'll get you a second one to cover the back so you're not flashing everyone your bum. Mrs. Carter down the hall might not be able to handle it. She's ninety if she's a day and a former Sunday school teacher to boot."

"Yeah, blame a poor little old lady."

Chloe pointed toward the word she'd spelled out again. "Like I said, ornery."

"I like to think of it as entertaining."

She huffed a little laugh. "I'm sure you do." She headed for the door. "Be right back. Do not get out of that bed or I'll tie you to it."

She was in full-on "I'm the doctor, do what I say" mode, but he had a flash of being tied to a bed for an entirely different purpose. He wasn't into that kind of stuff, but damn if what his hospital gown hid didn't react to the mental image.

"Yes, ma'am." He shot her a salute then pulled the blanket back over his lap, hoping she didn't notice how his body was reacting because how the hell was he supposed to explain that?

He closed his eyes and imagined being in an ice-cold shower, diving into the waters of the Arctic, sitting on a giant ice cube. Thankfully, it worked enough that by the time Chloe came back with one of the nurses, he wasn't in danger of embarrassing himself.

Chloe stepped to the side of his bed. "We're going to go slowly, okay?"

Damned if that didn't make him imagine being in bed with her, taking his time.

Ice water, ice water, ice water.

"Yeah," he said past the mantra repeating in his head.

The nurse pulled the IV pole out from where it sat near the head of the bed, while Chloe placed one hand on his shoulder and offered her other to him to grasp. The moment he wrapped his hand around her smaller one, he realized how very rough his was. It wasn't really something he'd ever considered when he'd touched a woman, but he found himself hoping he didn't mar her delicate skin.

He kept the blanket on his lap as Chloe tightened her grip and gradually helped him to a sitting position on the side of the bed. Despite the fact he had to convince her he was ready to leave the hospital, and his mounting medical debt, he couldn't suppress a groan when the muscles around his injuries protested loudly. Neither could he prevent the sweat that broke out on his lip and down his neck at the effort.

"Tell us if you feel like you can't do it," Chloe said.

Oh, hell no. He wasn't stopping now. "I'm good, Caitlin."

"Nope, still not it."

He saw the curious look the nurse turned toward Chloe.

"He's trying to guess my first name, so don't tell him."

"Okay," the nurse said slowly, as if she thought they were both odd. She unfurled the second gown and helped him slip it onto his shoulders so it covered his backside.

"Thanks," he said, smiling at the nurse whose name tag read Amanda. "Was feeling drafty back there."

"Think you can stop flirting with Amanda long enough to stand up?" Chloe asked.

He shifted his attention toward Chloe. "Would you rather I flirt with you, Camilla?"

She propped one of her hands on her hip. "Really? I look like a Camilla to you?"

He smiled wide. "It's better than some of the names I thought of."

"Well, you'll have to save that stellar list for another day. You're out of guesses for today. Now, cowboy, let's get you on your feet."

His smile fell away as he pushed slowly to his feet. He hated that Chloe and Amanda had to support him on both sides, but damned if he wasn't wobbly.

"You're probably light-headed from lying down so long and the rush of pain from engaging your stomach muscles for the first time since surgery."

"I'm fine." He almost managed to sound convincing. Almost.

"And I'm the queen of Denmark."

"Lead on, Your Majesty."

"I'd swat you like I do my brothers, but there's that whole 'do no harm' thing and I'm afraid you'd topple over."

"Saved by the Hippocratic oath."

When she met his gaze, he saw the surprise in her eyes. He leaned forward a little.

"I'm full of surprises."

Chloe seemed uncharacteristically flustered for a moment before she glanced at Amanda, then back at him.

"Do you want to walk or not?"

Deciding not to push his luck, he nodded once. He took a step and had to bite down against the pain that sliced through his middle. But he wasn't about to give up that easily. So he took another step and another. A few more and he was out in the hallway. The moment he spotted the sliding doors at the end of the hallway, probably the entrance to the emergency room, he wanted to make a break for freedom. But as much as he wanted to flee outside, he had the horrible feeling that if he tried he'd collapse from the pain before he got there. And falling flat on his face probably wasn't going to do wonders for the healing process.

As if Chloe could read his mind and didn't trust him not to make a run for it, she guided him in the opposite direction. He winced when he twisted his torso.

"Doing good," Chloe said. "But don't push too hard."

He wanted to tell her to stop babying him, but he kept his mouth shut, instead focusing on how putting one foot in front of the other was taking him closer to getting out of this place.

"Okay, let's turn around," Chloe said after he'd taken a few more steps.

He stiffened. "No." He realized he'd said it too loudly when the other two nurses at the desk that sat in the middle of the horseshoe of rooms looked straight at him. He took a breath and forced a smile. "I'm doing okay. Let's keep going."

When he glanced at Chloe, close enough that he could see the flecks of brownish gold in her eyes, she looked as if she might overrule him. But then something changed in her expression, a softening, a hint of understanding.

"Okay, but don't go so far that you don't think you can make it back."

Still looking down into her eyes, and deciding he really liked them, he nodded.

She was the one to break eye contact, and if he weren't mistaken her cheeks had pinkened before she did so.

Wyatt smiled as he focused on the hallway ahead of him. So Dr. Chloe Brody wasn't as unflappable as she tried to appear. Good to know.

"Onward," he said. "I hear there's a Mrs. Carter I need to go flirt with."

Chloe laughed under her breath, and that made his smile grow even wider. As he started walking again, he was even more determined to get better…and soon. Because the moment he could stand on his own two feet and walk under his own power, he just might see what else he could do to make Chloe Brody blush.

Chapter Five

"So this is the handsome young man I keep hearing so much about?" Mrs. Carter said when she looked up from her knitting to see Wyatt leaning against her doorway, more out of breath than he'd likely ever admit.

Wyatt turned his gaze to Chloe, a mischievous glint in his eyes and a smile on his lips, lips she really, really shouldn't be looking at so much.

"Have you been talking about me?"

Chloe laughed a little. "Don't look at me. You must have a secret admirer."

Wyatt shifted his gaze back to Mrs. Carter. "Well, whoever it is can't possibly be as pretty as you."

Chloe would swear she saw Mrs. Carter blush from across the room. If she weren't careful, she was going to scorch her pale, aged cheeks.

Mrs. Carter pointed a knitting needle at Wyatt. "You're going to have to watch this one. He'll be charming every female in the building."

"Shh," Wyatt said. "You'll give away my secret. I aim to charm my way out of this place."

"What's going to get you out of here is to do what your doctor says, and I'm saying it's time to go back to your room."

"Don't worry," Wyatt said in a fake whisper to Mrs. Carter. "I'll sneak back when I can. And we'll blow this joint."

Mrs. Carter smiled. "I'll hold you to that."

"Okay, Mr. Jailbreak, let's go," Chloe said, guiding Wyatt back toward his room four doors down.

By the time they walked through the door, she could see the strain on Wyatt's face. Even so, he balked as she tried to steer him toward the bed.

"I'm going to sit in the chair for a while. I can't stand that bed another minute."

For a split second she considered arguing but then realized there was no point. As long as he wasn't in danger of collapsing and tearing open his stitches, it didn't make any difference if he were in the bed or the chair.

"Besides, we can really get this game going," he said as he nodded toward the Scrabble board.

Chloe and Amanda flanked him as he reached the chair, but they let him use his own strength to lower himself to a sitting position. If he'd been alone, Chloe got the feeling he might have let a few choice words fly. But once he was seated, his muscles that had tightened up all over his body relaxed.

"You do realize that I'm working, right?"

"It's a small hospital," he said. "Just swing by to play a turn whenever you can."

"You're right. It is a small hospital. But those aren't my only patients. I have a full day of office visits at the clinic next door."

"You know what they say about all work and no play."

"I also know that it's frowned upon when you don't pay your bills."

The teasing expression on his face fell away. "Valid point."

An unexpected regret bubbled up inside her. She hated how with a single sentence she'd erased his good mood. "But I can probably sneak over once or twice during the day. Just remember, I'm a whiz at this game and you asked for it."

A hint of a smile tugged at his lips again, and some of her regret eased.

"I think I can handle it."

Throughout the rest of the day, Chloe saw patients at the clinic as usual. What wasn't normal, however, was how distracted she felt and how she slipped out the side door next to the hospital at lunch and then twice more in the afternoon to play rounds of the Scrabble game with Wyatt. She had to admit, he was proving a stronger opponent than she'd expected.

When she came in to see he'd played the word *zombify* for thirty-six points, she scanned the room. "You hiding a dictionary around here somewhere?"

"Yeah, I ran out and bought one while you were gone."

"A phone with internet access?"

"My phone is in my truck, which I guess is still sitting at the fairgrounds. Unless my lucky streak has continued and someone stole it."

"Would you like your phone? Surely you need to check in with someone?"

Wyatt glanced away for a moment. "I do need to make a couple of calls."

"Where are your keys?"

He pointed toward the closet. "Liam Parrish brought by my gear bag."

"That was nice of him." But then, Liam was a nice guy. Since he'd married her friend India and moved his rodeo company to Blue Falls, she'd gotten to know him better. He wouldn't fit better into the town if he'd been born there.

At that thought, she glanced at Wyatt's profile and wondered if he'd like living in Blue Falls. When he turned his gaze back to her, she averted her eyes.

"Something wrong?"

She shook her head. "Just a long day. I've got a couple more appointments this afternoon, then I'll run over and get your phone."

"You don't have to do that."

She shrugged as she crossed to the closet. "It's not far from here, so it's no biggie."

"Thanks."

She nodded once as she dug in his duffel bag past a rope, a cowbell, a roll of athletic tape, a pair of gloves and a worn T-shirt. Finally, at the bottom of the bag she found the key ring that held two keys. One appeared to belong to the truck, the other probably to wherever he called home when he wasn't on the road.

As she walked back to the clinic, she wasn't paying attention to anything other than the weight of Wyatt's keys in her pocket. She was way too aware of them and that by taking them she was getting even more involved with a patient, one who would be on the road out of Blue Falls the moment she signed his discharge papers.

"Hey, Chloe."

When she looked up at the sound of her name, she barely caught herself before she let a curse word slip.

It was too late to avoid Verona Charles, so she smiled and continued on the path that would cross the other woman's.

"Been over to check on your new patient?" Verona asked.

Chloe did her best to play dumb. "New patient?"

"Wyatt Kelley, the bull rider who was injured the other night. From what I hear, he's quite a looker."

"Mr. Kelley is on my rounds. Luckily, the hospital isn't terribly busy right now. Only five other patients besides Mr. Kelley, including Ruth Carter."

"Oh, how is Ruth doing?"

"As well as can be expected." You could only do so much when someone was ninety years old and in congestive heart failure. "Tired, but she does a pretty good job of being upbeat."

That reminded her of how Wyatt had teased Mrs. Carter. It was good to hear the older woman laugh, and Chloe had to admit that his actions only made him more attractive.

And she so didn't need to be thinking about how good-looking and nice Wyatt was when she was standing in front of Verona, who took matchmaking very seriously. And didn't let little things like the guy living hundreds of miles away stop her.

Chloe took a couple of steps toward the clinic, but instead of going on her way, Verona slid her arm around Chloe's and walked beside her.

"So, is Mr. Kelley as good-looking as I hear?"

Chloe did her best to keep her heartbeat from kicking into high gear. Instead, she nodded back toward the hospital. "You're welcome to go judge for yourself. He'll probably be happy to have someone come talk to him."

"Oh, I doubt he wants to talk to a little old lady he doesn't know."

"He's already been flirting with Ruth, so you better stake a claim." Chloe smiled, hoping to fluster Verona by throwing a bit of matchmaking back at her.

Verona patted Chloe's arm as they reached the entrance to the clinic. They stepped to the side to let Harry Beaman pass by with his rolling walker.

"I was thinking more about you, dear." Verona wasn't letting anything veer her away from her intended purpose for long. She was like a bloodhound who'd gotten a whiff of physical attraction in the air.

Chloe placed her hand atop Verona's. "I know what you're up to, and let me stop you right there. Mr. Kelley is a patient, nothing more."

"Not yet." That twinkle in Verona's eyes was dangerous.

"Not everyone has to be paired up. This isn't Noah's Ark, you know."

"But look how happy India and Liam are, and Skyler and Logan, Elissa and Pete." Verona took a breath, as if she were going to launch into another list of pairings she'd successfully orchestrated.

"What about you? Maybe it's time we find you a happily ever after."

Verona looked startled by the suggestion. "Oh, honey, I'm too old for that."

Chloe took a step back and propped her hands on her hips, trying her best to ignore Wyatt's keys when she bumped them. "Verona Charles, you are not old. You've got more energy than a lot of people half your age."

Some of the vitality seeped out of Verona's expression, replaced by a tinge of what looked like sadness. "I've had my chance."

"Ever heard of second chances?"

"I'm not here to talk about me."

"Listen, I'm touched that you care enough about me to want to see me happy, but I am. I love my job, have a good relationship with my family, am lucky to have lots of friends and live in one of the prettiest places in the world. I couldn't ask for anything more."

Even as the words left her mouth, they didn't feel like the truth. Down deep, she did want more. At least she was beginning to think she did. But her life had been filled with responsibilities and work for so long, she wasn't sure if she even knew what kind of guy she'd want. Would she realize it if she stumbled across him? For some reason, her hand itched to curl around Wyatt's keys, but she refrained.

"We all crave love."

Chloe touched Verona's shoulder. "And I have lots of love in my life. Now, if you'll excuse me, I've probably got a patient waiting on me."

With a quick smile, Chloe headed inside. But instead of going straight for her office, she detoured to the restroom. After the encounter with Verona, she needed a minute alone to purge thoughts of Wyatt and how her thoughts kept drifting to him as Verona had sang the praises of coupledom.

She stared into the mirror and shook her head. Why was she even letting Verona get to her? Chloe didn't have time for a relationship even if she did spot someone she liked. Between her hours at the clinic, the hospital and taking care of her family, when did she have time for anything more than the occasional casual date? Was there a part of her that was a bit jealous when she saw how crazy in love her friends were with their husbands or fiancés? Of course, she was only human. But that was the point. There were a limited number of hours in the day, and most of hers were filled.

If she wanted Verona to believe her when she said she felt nothing for Wyatt beyond the concern a doctor has for a patient, she needed to stop running over to see him every time she had two minutes to spare. Because though she'd never admit it to Verona, or anyone else for that matter, it wasn't the thrill of the Scrabble game that kept her going back. Only to herself could she admit she had a little crush on Wyatt. But who wouldn't? He was tall, nicely built, tanned from time outside, had that type of chiseled face that she liked. That he possessed a sense of humor and a casual flirtiness didn't hurt.

She just had to make sure she didn't let herself get too deep into the crush because when he was discharged from the hospital, Wyatt didn't have any reason to stay in Blue Falls. He wouldn't be healed enough to ride in the upcoming rodeos, so he might as well go home to recuperate. And maybe then Verona would shift her focus to someone else. Of course, she might simply look for another potential match for Chloe.

Shoving all those concerns aside, she took a deep breath and headed for her office. Toward an afternoon of blessed normalcy.

But when she entered an examination room a few minutes later to see India Parrish and her baby daughter, a wave of longing for a child of her own hit her from out of nowhere. Sure, little Rose was adorable, but it was far from the first time Chloe had seen her. Rose had made her appearance in the world six weeks early, so Chloe had kept a close eye on her since her birth. She'd even held her on a few occasions. Why did the mere sight of her in her mother's arms twist Chloe up in maternal knots now?

"You okay, Chloe?" India asked.

"Uh, yeah. Sorry, my train of thought derailed there for a minute."

"I know that feeling, though I think mine is from a distinct lack of sleep."

Chloe smiled as she crossed the small room. "That sounds normal." She leaned over and bopped the baby gently on her sweet button nose. "And how are you today, Miss Rose?"

The big smile Rose gave her lit up the room and made Chloe yearn to hug her close and inhale that sweet baby scent.

Making it through Rose's regular checkup proved more difficult than it should have been. In fact, after Chloe finished with her last appointment of the day, she headed straight home. It wasn't until she walked in the front door that she remembered Wyatt's keys in her pocket. She pulled them out and considered going back into town but nixed that idea in favor of a long, hot bath. He'd lived this long without his phone. What was one more day?

She, however, needed the time to purge her mind of him, of how there was a sliver inside of her that wanted to encourage Verona's efforts rather than protesting them. But as she sank down into the bath and let the warmth soak into her tired body, she realized what was happening. As if someone had turned on a switch, her maternal clock had started ticking. And Wyatt Kelley just happened to be the first attractive, available guy she'd seen after the ticking had started.

At least that was the story she told herself as she drifted near sleep and tried to banish thoughts of Wyatt joining her in the tub.

WYATT STARED AT the printout of his hospital bill he'd asked Sophie to bring him that morning. No matter how many times he looked at it, the numbers didn't get any smaller. The total he owed after insurance was more than he made in a year, and that number was only going to increase every day he stayed in this hospital.

He eyed the Scrabble board with the unfinished game. He'd expected Chloe to come back for one more turn before she'd gone home the night before, but she hadn't. Logic told him she'd been tired and had forgotten and that it shouldn't matter to him. But until she showed up again with his truck keys, he was stuck. Maybe that had been her plan all along.

Movement at the doorway drew his attention, but his hope deflated when he saw an older, gray-haired doctor enter the room.

"Good morning, Mr. Kelley. I'm Dr. Hershel. How are you feeling?"

"Ready to get out of here."

Dr. Hershel nodded. "I hear a lot of that."

"So when can I leave?"

"That'll be up to Dr. Pierce and Dr. Brody. I'm just filling in this morning."

"For Dr. Brody?"

"Yeah, she's got a full house at the clinic. Oh, she asked me to give you these." Dr. Hershel reached into the pocket of his white coat and pulled out Wyatt's cell phone and truck keys.

Well, Chloe must be done humoring him—all the more reason to get back on the road. When he'd walked down the hall yesterday, his side and stomach had hurt like the devil. But all he had to manage was to get outside and hitch a ride to his truck. He'd sat in the chair for several hours the day before so he could manage sitting on his butt as he drove. Where the hell he was going to go, he had no idea. No sense driving all the way back to Laramie, but even he now realized he wasn't going to be riding for the next few events.

He cursed under his breath.

"Excuse me?"

Wyatt met the older doctor's eyes. He seemed like a nice enough guy, but he wasn't Chloe. "Nothing."

Yeah, he needed to get out of Blue Falls before he did something really stupid and made Chloe think more was going on than some meaningless flirting.

He waited until Dr. Hershel was gone before he swung his feet over the side of the bed. A sharp pain skewered his middle, and not for the first time he called that bull a string of unflattering names.

When he was able to catch his breath and be sure his face wasn't reflecting the pain he was in, he hit the nurse-call button on the side of the bed. He listened as the squeak of rubber-soled shoes came nearer before Sophie stepped into the room.

"You need something?"

He lifted his arm. "Yeah, you to take this IV out."

Her forehead wrinkled. "Dr. Hershel didn't say anything about that."

"I'm leaving. I'm guessing you'd like me to leave the IV pole here."

"You're leaving against medical advice?"

"If that's what it takes. I can't stay cooped up in here forever. I'm going stir-crazy." He wasn't about to admit that it was because he couldn't stop imagining his bill ticking steadily upward like the numbers on a gas pump. He didn't want her or anyone else thinking that he wasn't going to pay what he owed. It was just going to take a while, and nothing was getting paid while he lounged around attached to monitors and an IV.

"Let me go call Dr. Brody."

"No, she's busy."

But Sophie was already halfway out the door.

"Damn it." He clenched his teeth then ripped the IV out himself. He pressed a towel against the trickle of blood as he crossed to the door and shut it. By the time he got to the closet, he was questioning his sanity. But he hadn't been lying. Even with Chloe's visits, he was beginning to feel the institutional walls close in on him. He needed to breathe fresh air, soak in the warmth of the sun on his face, not feel as trapped as he would in prison.

He froze for a moment at that thought before hurrying as best he could to change out of the hospital gown and into his regular clothes. By the time he got his jeans pulled carefully over his bandages, he was sweating and light-headed. He grabbed his boots and held on to the bed as he walked toward the chair.

The way he felt, he wouldn't be surprised if he looked down to find himself cut into two halves.

For a scary moment, he feared he'd never heal,

would never climb onto the back of a bull again. He let out a breath, trying to push those thoughts away. Because without his riding, who the hell was he?

Chapter Six

Chloe retrieved a patient chart from outside an examination room and was about to open the door when Jenna came rushing down the hallway.

"Chloe, you need to get over to the hospital. Wyatt Kelley just ripped his own IV out and is attempting to leave the hospital."

"Damn it." That fool was going to injure himself all over again.

She handed the chart to Jenna and ran toward the exit. The moment she stepped into the hospital, Angie, the X-ray tech, pointed down the hallway that led out through the ER. As soon as Chloe turned the corner, she saw Wyatt heading away from her, his hand propped against the wall to steady himself. Sophie was walking backward beside him, likely trying to get him to reconsider.

Chloe shook her head and went after her patient. She walked past him then turned and parked herself in his path and crossed her arms. "Just where do you think you're going?"

"Home."

"Mighty long drive to Wyoming for a guy who can't even walk without assistance from the wall."

Wyatt pressed his lips together and brought his hand down to his side. "You can't keep me here against my will."

Chloe cocked her head slightly. "Did something happen? You seemed fine yesterday." Surely her absence last night and this morning hadn't pushed him over the edge. No, something else was going on, something he wasn't saying.

"I just need to get out of this place."

She mentally pulled back the layers of what he said. Beyond the need to be outside, what would be bothering a guy like him? Then it clicked. He was a bull rider on a smaller circuit, one who couldn't ride now. No riding meant no income. And hospital bills didn't come cheap.

"Okay, I'll tell you what. Let's go sit outside for a while. Maybe you'll feel better if you absorb a little sun and get some fresh air."

The look he gave her was full of suspicion, and she couldn't blame him for looking that way. Even to a casual observer, she doubted she came across as a person who gave up that easily.

Chloe glanced at Sophie. "It's okay. I think Mr. Kelley and I can handle it from here."

Sophie looked at Wyatt briefly before she nodded and headed in the opposite direction.

Chloe positioned herself next to Wyatt and patted her shoulder. "Hold on to me. I can't have you toppling over. We frown on guts on the clean floors."

In contrast to his demeanor a moment before, he huffed a small laugh at that.

"Well, look at that," she said. "The guy with a sense of humor is still in there."

He didn't respond, and she could tell it was because he was concentrating all his effort into not showing how much he was hurting. She slowly guided him out through the sliding ER doors and to a small courtyard off to the right. By the time they reached one of the benches, she could almost feel his pain herself. She had to give him credit. He might be as stubborn as the proverbial mule, but he was also tough. And not just physically. Somewhere along the way, Wyatt Kelley had perfected a mental toughness, too.

When he was seated and had dropped his bag on the ground beside him, she sank onto the opposite bench and looked up at the bright blue April sky. "You're right. It is nicer out here."

"You didn't happen to bring my truck here, did you?"

She let her gaze drift back down to his. "No. And no matter how determined you are, I don't think you'll make it all the way to the fairgrounds."

"I'll catch a ride."

"Because everybody picks up a stranger on the side of the road."

"I'll manage."

Chloe sighed and leaned forward. "Listen, I understand you're not going to go back inside, no matter what I say. But you're also in no shape to be on your own yet. You are on strong pain meds, still healing and in danger of reopening your wounds, at risk of infection if the wounds don't receive proper care. You don't need to drive quite yet, and you'll need someone to help you for at least a while."

Wyatt ran his hand down over his face. "That's not an option."

"You've got to meet me partway."

He fixed his gaze on hers. "I can't. There isn't anyone, no family, no one who isn't on the road."

Wyatt seemed so matter-of-fact that it broke her heart. She still had a hole where her mother had been, but she couldn't imagine having no one, not a single soul to take care of her when she couldn't take care of herself. She'd never known anyone that alone, and she was helpless to stop the sudden urge to do something about it.

Before she could consider how crazy it sounded, she said, "Then I guess you're coming home with me."

Wyatt stared at the doctor, wondering if he'd passed out somewhere back in the hospital and was imagining this entire conversation. "What?"

Chloe looked surprised by her own words but then leaned back and stretched out her arms along the back of the bench. "If you're not going to behave and stay here then you have to stay somewhere until you're really able to be on your own."

"So you're offering to take a man you barely know to your home?"

She smiled. "I'm pretty sure you're no threat to me in your current condition."

He shook his head. "You've got to work."

"Yes, I do, which is why you'll do exactly what I say."

"Anyone ever tell you that you're bossy?"

"Frequently."

"I appreciate your offer, but I need to get on the road."

"To where?"

He had no idea, and from the look on her face she knew that. She was too damn perceptive. "California. There's a rodeo in a couple of weeks. I'll get there, rest, then be ready to ride."

"Seriously? You think you're going to be able to ride a bull in two weeks?"

"I'll see when the time comes."

"Listen, I know you rodeo riders are all tough guys, ride injured and all that macho stuff. But your injuries aren't something a little tape and some ibuprofen can fix. You ride anytime soon and you're risking even more extensive damage than you had this time."

"I can't just sit around doing nothing. I've got to work."

"I know it sucks, but that doesn't change the facts. You get on a bull anytime in the near future, and you will regret it."

Wyatt typically kept his emotions inside, but at the moment he wanted nothing more than to scream. Damned if he could see another way out of his current situation. Despite his assertion that he'd be okay on his own, already the pain in his middle was worse than when he'd nearly collapsed onto the bench. He hated to depend on anyone else. Too often they failed you when you needed them most. But this was temporary, and there were worse places to stay than at the home of one very pretty doctor.

"Fine, but I earn my keep."

She shook her head once. "I've had my share of stubborn patients before, but you're rushing right to the top of the list. You'll earn your keep by resting, getting better so you don't end up right back here. I mean, I know it's your favorite place—"

"Oh, no, you don't," she said as she hurried up next to him. "No bending or picking up anything over five pounds."

"I'm not an invalid."

"And you're not in top shape, either. Remember, the deal is you do what I say."

Wyatt made a sound of frustration deep in his throat, and Chloe had to turn away to hide her smile.

When she got him in the car, she tossed his bag into the backseat before rounding to the driver's side. "I don't know about you, but I'm hungry. For some reason, I missed my lunch break."

"Probably because you interrupted someone's clean getaway."

She laughed. "That had to be the slowest getaway ever." She couldn't help but snort out another laugh. "I'm sorry. I know your pain isn't funny."

Chloe managed to clamp down on her laughter by focusing on the street in front of her as she pulled away from the hospital.

"I suppose it was a bit like a snail trying to make a run for it, wasn't it?"

Chloe lost it all over again and only got her laughter under control when she pulled up in front of the Primrose Café. "So, you want fried chicken or brisket?"

"Brisket. Look in my bag. My wallet is in there."

She waved away his suggestion.

"I can pay for my own lunch," he said, his laughter gone. "I'm not a charity case."

"I'm aware. I'll make you a deal. When you get better, you buy me lunch."

"Who's being stubborn now?"

She smiled at him, something she realized was easy

He held up a hand. "I get the point."

"Finally." Then she smiled, and something inside him did an odd little flip.

"I guess at least I'll have a chance to beat you in our Scrabble game."

"Yeah, not gonna happen."

Though his pain level was ratcheting up by the second, he smiled.

"If I leave you sitting here, am I going to get a call in two minutes that you're hobbling your way down Main Street?"

"I'm not going anywhere."

Chloe stood. "That's more like it. I'll take care of all the discharge paperwork and get you some medicine for the pain."

He wanted to deny he was hurting, but he knew she'd be able to tell he was lying. If he knew anything about Chloe Brody, it was that she was good at her job. And so dedicated that she was willing to take a virtual stranger home to make sure he healed to her satisfaction.

"YOU'RE DOING WHAT?" Sophie asked a few minutes later as Chloe filled out the necessary paperwork to release Wyatt from the hospital.

"It's no big deal. He has nowhere to go, no one to take care of him while he gets better."

"So you're taking him home with you? I was right, wasn't I? You've got the hots for him."

"Oh, don't be silly. I'm his doctor. I wouldn't be a very good one if I allowed him to do himself further injury, would I?"

Sophie leaned her hip against the side of the desk

inside the nurses' station. "I think Verona got to you, made you realize you had the perfect man right under your nose."

"I swear there is something weird in the water around here." Chloe propped one hand on her hip. "He's been here a few days. Verona hasn't even met him. No one could possibly know whether he's perfect for anyone. All we know is that he is a bull rider, easily bored, plays a decent game of Scrabble and is contrary."

"And he's good-looking."

"You have a one-track mind."

"Well, he is."

Chloe rolled her eyes and signed the last of the discharge forms.

"Really, Chloe. I don't know any other doctor who would take a patient home with them."

"Well, I don't make a habit out of it, but what am I supposed to do? From what I can tell, he's got no family to take care of him." She glanced over her shoulder to make sure Wyatt hadn't by some miracle wandered back inside. "Guys like him, they pretty much live winning paycheck-to-winning paycheck. And if they can't ride or are on a losing streak, things can get pretty thin. Owen said he knew a roper who was so down on his luck that he was living in a tent."

Sophie shook her head. "That's it. I didn't even think."

"What?"

"He asked me to get a printout of his bill this morning. Maybe I shouldn't have done that."

"No, it's not your fault. He probably had a good idea it was a sizable amount already or he wouldn't have asked for it. Plus, I think he's just at his limit for being in here."

He certainly wasn't the first patient to check himself out because he couldn't stand the inside of the hospital anymore. If she had unlimited funds at her disposal, she would design and build a new type of hospital that felt more like being at home with movies at the push of a button, gaming systems, big windows with beautiful views. But she didn't have that kind of dough, so it was a waste of time dreaming about it. She'd be happy if people just took better care of themselves so they wouldn't have to go into the hospital in the first place.

After taking care of Wyatt's discharge, she hurried back to the clinic to get her purse and to tell Jenna to either reschedule her remaining appointments or shift them to Dr. Hershel or Dr. Carrington.

"What's going on?"

Chloe pressed her palm against her forehead, wondering if she were crazy for what she was about to do. "Long story. I'll tell you later, or Sophie can catch you up. I'll be back in the morning."

"Okay."

Not giving herself time to think that perhaps she was making a mistake, Chloe headed for her car. She thought about calling her dad or one of her brothers to give them a heads-up but imagined how that conversation would go. So, yeah, she was just going to show up with an injured stranger in tow. After all, her family was less likely to balk if Wyatt were already there.

When she pulled around to the ER entrance, she was glad to see Wyatt was still upright. By the time she got out of the car, he was already on his feet and about to bend over to grab his bag.

to do. "You must be rubbing off on me." Before he could argue further about who was picking up the tab, she hopped out of the car and hurried across the street.

After she ordered, her gaze landed on the pie offerings for the day. "Add a couple slices of lemon pie to that, Daisy."

"You got it."

"The hospital cafeteria not hitting the spot today?"

Chloe did her best to paste on an expression of casual normalcy before she glanced over to find Verona standing next to her. She leaned a little toward the older woman. "It's mystery meat day." She threw in a shudder for effect.

Daisy picked that moment to place the bag holding the obvious two containers of food along with the twin slices of pie down in front of Chloe.

"You must have skipped breakfast," Verona said.

Chloe pretended not to hear as she handed the money to Daisy and said, "Keep the change." Chances were Verona had already spotted Wyatt sitting in her car outside and was basking in the idea that her matchmaking mojo had been successful again. Even though Verona was wrong, Chloe wasn't about to argue. Doing so would just make Verona more determined. Better not to feed the fire.

She grabbed the bag and turned to leave. "Gotta run. Have a good afternoon."

"You, too."

Yep, there was a little too much self-satisfaction in those two words.

"Something wrong?" Wyatt asked as she pulled out of the parking lot back onto Main Street.

"No, why?"

"You seemed preoccupied when you came back."

"Oh, it's nothing. Work stuff."

"If you need to go back to work, I can just sit in the car until you're done."

"No, I'm good until tomorrow morning."

Even though Chloe felt she was doing the right thing, and didn't really see another option other than not caring what happened to Wyatt, a nervous flutter started in her stomach. And it got worse the closer she got to the ranch.

"Pretty country out here," Wyatt said, making her realize he hadn't said anything in the past two or three miles.

"Yeah, I'd say we lucked out and got the prettiest part of Texas. And you're here during our best time." She pointed out the windshield at the wildflowers lining the side of the road.

"I saw a bus go by while you were in the café. People really pay to go on wildflower tours?"

"Loads of them. Blue Falls's economy revolves around wildflowers. The regular rodeos are a nice draw, too, but they're new enough that Liam is still in building mode with them."

When Chloe made the turn into the ranch, she realized she wasn't going to be able to get Wyatt settled in the house before she had to give her family the news that they were going to have a houseguest for a while. Seeing as how her brothers, dad and even Emmett, one of the ranch hands, were gathered outside the barn, it looked as if the news breaking was happening now.

"You don't live by yourself." It wasn't a question.

"No, there's four of us. Me, Dad and my two brothers."

"Do they know they're about to have company?"

"Nope, but don't worry. They'll understand."

At least she hoped they would. Only one way to find out.

As she stepped out of the car, she saw her dad approaching and went to meet him.

"You're home early," he said. "Is something wrong?"

"No, just took a half day."

"That's not like you."

For some reason, his response bothered her. Lots of people took half days on occasion. Why couldn't she? She shook off what was most likely an imagined criticism and motioned toward the car, where Wyatt was opening his door.

"We're going to have a guest for a while."

"Oh?"

She glanced over her shoulder in time to see the tight lines of pain on Wyatt's face as he pulled himself to his feet. "Dad, this is Wyatt Kelley. He needs a bit more time to recuperate before he's able to drive and be out on his own. Wyatt, this is my dad, Wayne Brody."

"Good to meet you, sir."

Her dad nodded at Wyatt then lowered his voice so that only Chloe could hear. "Isn't that what the hospital is for?"

"He checked himself out."

"So you brought him here?" Her dad's forehead creased below his well-worn hat.

Chloe kept her voice quiet, as well, not wanting to embarrass Wyatt. "He doesn't have anyone, Dad. Nowhere to go, no one to help."

Her dad let out a long breath. "Girl, sometimes I think your heart is too big."

"What's going on?"

Chloe looked past her dad to where Garrett and Owen were approaching.

"Your sister's brought home a guest."

She caught movement out of the corner of her eye. Wyatt had made his way to the front of her car, but looked as if he might pass out at any moment. Before she could say anything else, Wyatt extended his hand toward Garrett.

"Wyatt Kelley. Sorry to intrude like this, but your sister refused to believe I'd be fine on my own."

Chloe caught herself right before assuring him that he wouldn't. It was one thing to say it when it was just him and her, another entirely when he was trying to save face in front of other guys. She'd grown up around enough testosterone to know when to push and when not.

Wyatt shook Garrett's hand then her father's. Before he could turn toward Owen, however, her younger brother started laughing.

"What the devil has gotten into you?" she asked.

Garrett gave Owen a slight punch in the upper arm, a big-brother gesture meant to silently tell him to behave.

"What?" Owen said. "You've got to admit it's funny. I mean, she's been bringing home injured animals for years, but it's the first time the stray has been a man."

Chloe felt heat rush up her throat to flood her face. She stared hard and narrowed her eyes at her younger brother, letting him know that the first chance she got, he was toast.

Damn if that didn't just make him laugh all the harder.

Chapter Seven

Wyatt hadn't felt as trapped as he did now since he was a kid. He was miles away from his truck and escape, stuck at the home of a doctor who was annoyingly right about him not being 100 percent, and she'd forgotten to mention she still lived with her dad and brothers. To top it all off, one of those brothers was finding Wyatt's unexpected appearance at their front door hilarious.

"I can get a motel room in town." And as soon as he was able to climb into his truck without feeling as if he were going to pass out from the pain and Chloe left him alone, he'd hit the road and not look back.

"Pay no attention to my idiot brother," Chloe said.

"Hey, I take exception to that." Then her brother turned to Wyatt and extended his hand. "Owen Brody. Don't mind my sister. She thinks she's the boss."

Wyatt glanced at Chloe, who looked as if she might rip off her brother's head at any moment. "I noticed."

Chloe shifted her gaze to him, her mouth dropping open a little. She glanced at Owen then back to him and shook her head. "You are two pain-in-the-butt peas in a pod."

Wyatt made eye contact with Owen. "Does she treat all her patients like this?"

"Okay, that's enough picking on me," she said. "Let's get you inside."

As she made a move to take his arm to help him, he stepped past her and headed for the front steps. No way was he going to look like an invalid in front of her family. He didn't want them thinking he'd be mooching their hospitality a moment longer than necessary.

By the time he reached the top of the steps, sweat was running like a river down the middle of his back and his head swam. All his determination to appear on the mend would go straight down the toilet if he ended up passing out and falling backward down the stairs. Knowing his luck, he'd probably break his neck this time.

To her credit, Chloe didn't attempt to aid him when she climbed up to his side. She did open the door and hold it for him, but he could believe she'd do that for anyone. But one look at her slightly raised brow told him that she knew exactly how close he was to doubling over.

When they stepped inside the living room of her home, something felt off about it. He couldn't figure out how he could possibly know that, and there was nothing obviously wrong with the comfortable-looking space. But something just felt...wrong. Even so, he was grateful to be somewhere that didn't look and feel institutional, like the inside of a bottle of disinfectant.

"I think you've had just about enough excitement for one day," Chloe said when she closed the door behind him, leaving everyone else outside.

He wanted to argue but couldn't. The pain was increasing by the moment, and he didn't want to embarrass himself by pushing too hard. "I could use a pain pill."

"And a nap."

"A nap? That sounds like something kindergart-ners do."

"Some sleep, rest, z's, whatever you want to call it. You want to get better, and sometimes what your body needs to heal is sleep."

Not allowing him time to respond even if he could think of something to say, she turned and headed for a hallway that likely led to the bedrooms. With a grunt he hoped she didn't hear, he followed her. When he stepped into the bedroom, he knew it was her room. It wasn't that it was pink and frilly, but the framed pictures of wildflowers lining one wall didn't seem like something her dad or brothers would have in their rooms. Neither was the white wooden desk and chair angled in one corner, or the floor-to-ceiling bookcase crammed with what looked like a collection of medi-cal thrillers, thick textbooks and titles about Texas.

"This is your room," he said.

"Observant."

"Shouldn't I be in the guest room?"

"Don't have one, not once my brothers got old enough that sharing a room was decidedly uncool. Plus, they didn't think it was fair that I had my own room just because I was the only girl."

"I can't take your room. I'll sleep on the couch."

She propped one hand on her hip. "You're going to fight me every step of the way, aren't you?"

"Not fighting. I don't need all this room, just some-where to sleep at night."

Chloe turned more fully toward him. "You want to get better as quickly as you can, right?"

"Yes." He doubted anything could be more obvious.

"Then you need to rest whenever your body says it needs rest. And for that, you need your own space. I'm gone most of every day anyway, and busy doing other stuff even when I'm home."

He wanted to argue further, but it was useless. And the longer he balked at the sleeping arrangements, the longer it was going to take to get that pain pill, the one he didn't want but needed. He was beginning to feel as if his gut were ripping open again.

Not verbally admitting defeat, he nonetheless walked over to the bed that was covered with a light green comforter and sat on the side. "At least the bed isn't covered in flowers."

Chloe laughed. "Yes, because they might attack you and you'd lose macho points." She shook her head. "Guys are weird."

"Guys? No, girls are definitely the weirder of the two sexes."

"I guess we'll just have to agree to disagree. Now lie back and let me check your dressings. I want to make sure you haven't popped any stitches with all your gallivanting around today."

Before doing as she instructed, he shoved off his boots. As he lay back on the soft bed—heaven compared to that torture device at the hospital—he couldn't help the moan of pain.

"You overdid it today," Chloe said as she lifted his shirt as if it were no big deal and pulled off the bandages.

"Not the first time I've done something stupid. Won't be the last."

"Admitting stupidity is always the first step."

He laughed, which made his injuries hurt more but was worth it because it made her smile, too. Here, without the hospital as the backdrop, Chloe Brody was even prettier. He had to fight the urge to lift his hand and run his fingers over her cheek to see if it were as soft as it looked.

"I suppose I should tell you my name since you're staying at my house." She applied some sort of medicine to his incisions, probably antibiotic cream.

"Chloe," he said.

She glanced up at him. "Good guess."

He smiled.

"Wait. Someone told you, didn't they?"

"I might have asked."

Her eyes narrowed a fraction. "When?"

"Several days ago."

"But you've been guessing the wrong names."

"I had to make sure you came back every day."

The look of surprise on her face made him want to frame her face with his hands and kiss her. But that was a very bad idea. Injured or not, he was pretty sure her dad and brothers would frown on him accosting her in her own bedroom.

For the first time since they'd met, she seemed flustered and didn't have a snappy comeback as she finished applying new bandages. "Your pain meds are in the car. Be back in a minute."

As she started to step away, without thinking he reached out and grabbed her hand. "Thanks."

He wasn't sure if he was thanking her for the medicine, for giving him an alternative to the hospital, or simply for caring more about him than most people in his life ever had. It didn't matter why he said it. He just knew he needed to.

She didn't ask what he meant, only nodded before walking out of the room.

EVEN THOUGH SHE'D taken half a day off from work, Chloe was exhausted by the time she put dinner on the table that night. Since an unusually cool rain had moved in midafternoon, she'd gone with chicken and dumplings.

She hated to bother Wyatt since he'd evidently given in to the rest she'd insisted he needed. But to get better, he also needed to eat. She'd taken a few steps toward the hall when she heard a door open. At the same moment, the back door also swung open, and her dad and brothers filed into the mudroom. One glance at their boots told her that the room would live up to its name tonight.

Garrett was the first one to come into the kitchen, and his gaze immediately scanned his surroundings, as if he thought Wyatt might have slit her throat or something. "Our guest conked out already?"

"He's been sleeping all afternoon, but I just heard him get up."

Garrett walked to the sink to wash his hands then turned to look at her as he dried them on a towel. "Do you think this is a good idea?"

Chloe heard another door close, followed by the sound of running water. "I'm just doing my job."

"I'm pretty sure most doctors don't bring their patients home, especially when they barely know them. You sure there's nothing else going on?"

She stopped filling bowls with dumplings and

turned halfway to look at him. "What's that supposed to mean?"

"He's a decent-looking guy, and you're single."

She laughed. "You think I've got a thing for him?"

"Do you?"

A hot denial was on her lips, but she found she couldn't say the words. "Like you said, I barely know him." Which wasn't exactly a denial of attraction, but she hoped her brother didn't realize that.

When Owen walked past her toward the table, he was wearing a grin so full of mischief that Chloe wanted to throttle him. She remembered his teasing about Wyatt a few days before and realized she'd given him more ammunition for his theory.

Thankfully, she was saved from more teasing when Wyatt eased his way into the kitchen.

"Evening," her father said to him. "You're looking better than you were earlier."

"Amazing what sleep in a real bed and a couple pain pills can do."

As Chloe carried the final two bowls to the table, it hit her that Wyatt had nowhere to sit. That fact seemed to occur to her dad and brothers at the same time, and they all went quiet and still. Before Wyatt could ask what was wrong, she directed him to the chair she normally sat in.

"Be right back." She didn't make eye contact with anyone as she walked into the pantry and grabbed one of the extra chairs, but not the one her mother used to sit in. Even though they'd used it since her mother's death when they had enough company for a meal to warrant it, most of the time the reminder of her absence was kept out of sight. She paused long enough to rub her fingertips along the back of her mother's chair, a match for all the others except for the dent in the top slat of the back where her mom had dropped a hot casserole dish. Though memories of her mom could still make her sad, this time she smiled.

Not wanting to leave the guys in awkward silence, she grabbed the other chair and walked back into the kitchen. Her dad and Garrett were at their normal spots at the opposite ends of the table, and damn if Owen wasn't already parked in his chair, firmly planted in the middle of the table opposite Wyatt. A hint of a smile tugged at the edges of his mouth.

Before she could tell Owen to move his butt, Wyatt scooted his chair to the side, giving her room to place hers next to his. Pretending that nothing was awkward about the situation, she slid into her spot.

She hadn't considered that having Wyatt at the table might put a damper on their normal routine, but suddenly she grasped for something to say.

"So, Wyatt, I hear you're from Wyoming," her dad said. "I've been up that way once. Got a friend who has a spread up near the Big Horns. Pretty country."

"Yes, sir, it is. Awful cold in the winter, though."

Her dad chuckled. "It is that."

Chloe breathed a little easier as the conversation flowed into a back-and-forth about the ranch, Wyatt's year so far on the circuit and the latest news about the fence cutters.

"They're not taking any of the cattle?" Wyatt asked.

"No," her dad said. "Just doing it for pure meanness."

Chloe relaxed as the meal progressed. Wyatt's presence didn't seem like that big of a change, at least not until they both reached for a piece of bread at the same moment and their hands bumped. Chloe jerked hers back at the buzzy awareness that flared to life between them, which made no sense because she'd already seen him half-naked and thought nothing of it.

Okay, so that wasn't entirely true. She'd seen a lot of men's bare chests since becoming a doctor, most of which became a blur as soon as the patient was gone. But Wyatt Kelley's well-cut muscles were still there in her brain, inhabiting way too much real estate for her peace of mind.

She refused to let herself look at him, and instead reached for a napkin as if that were what she'd been after all along. By instinct, she also knew not to meet Owen's gaze across the table.

"So, Wyatt," Owen said. "How did Chloe convince you to come home with her?"

This time she did look up, shooting mental daggers at her brother. Owen just looked amused.

"Got tired of arguing." Wyatt glanced at her in the same moment she caved and looked at him. He smiled a little, and it made him impossibly sexier than he'd already been.

Yeah, she admitted it. Wyatt Kelley was sexy, the epitome of the American-cowboy fantasy. She'd grown up around lots of cowboys, but even she got sucked into the fantasy now and then. Like right now as they probably stared at each other for way too long, considering her dad and brothers were in the same room.

She forced herself to casually look away. "So, Owen, which unfortunate girl gets the pleasure of your company tonight?"

"I'm taking a night off. Figured things might be pretty interesting around here with company."

Chloe turned toward Wyatt. "Owen's bucket list includes dating every girl in the county and all the surrounding ones."

"And trying every profession under the sun," Garrett added, earning himself a kick under the table.

Chloe's father sighed. "Wyatt, I'm sorry. I tried to teach these three manners. As you can see, it didn't take so well."

Chloe and her brothers all protested at once, which was followed by a pause, then everyone at the table gave in to laughter.

"I'm not sure about your dates," Wyatt said to Owen. "But this is definitely more interesting than the night-life at the hospital."

A snort escaped Chloe before she could catch it, which led to even more laughter from all around.

Wyatt held up his hand and tried to hide a grimace. "Don't make me laugh."

"Sucks to be you, man," Owen said.

Wyatt nodded. "Tell me about it."

After dinner, the guys headed for the living room. Wyatt lingered in the doorway as Chloe heard the TV click on.

"You need any help?"

"I'm good," she said. "You should go get off your feet."

"I've been off my feet most of the day."

"Good."

He shook his head. "Stubborn" was all he said before following in the wake of her dad and brothers.

But the way he said it, as if maybe he didn't mind

her stubbornness so much anymore, caused a flicker of happiness to come to life within her. She knew it wasn't wise, but that knowledge didn't seem to matter.

WYATT HATED HAVING his days and nights mixed up. After sleeping the day away, he found it difficult to sleep more than a few minutes at a time. Instead, he lay in Chloe's bed, surrounded by her fresh, feminine scent, thinking about what it'd be like if she were beside him.

She was not the kind of woman he tended to gravitate toward when he allowed himself to be with a woman at all. His encounters were usually one-time things with no strings attached. He wasn't anywhere near as bad as some guys on the circuit, but even he liked a woman warming his bed now and again.

But not Chloe. She was a good woman, caring, professional. Not to mention she lived with three guys who would likely have no problem finishing what Beelzebub started if he stepped out of line with her. Even though they hadn't come right out and said it, he got the feeling they were protective of her. He wondered if that had anything to do with her mother not being in the picture. He had no idea where the older woman was, if she were even still alive, but he'd caught the strained moment the night before when Chloe had realized there weren't enough chairs at the table.

Still, despite knowing all the reasons why he shouldn't, he found himself daydreaming about what it'd be like to pull Chloe close, to kiss her and find out if those pink lips tasted as sweet as they looked. He wondered whether she'd be interested in him if they knew each other better.

Of course not, because if she knew everything about

him, she'd likely want nothing to do with him. And he couldn't blame her.

Needing to think of anything other than something that could never be, he slowly lifted himself to the side of the bed and turned on the light. He took several moments to catch his breath.

Another pain pill sounded good, but he'd seen too many people get hooked on drugs of various types to want to take them for long. Might as well start weaning himself off them now, no matter how much his stomach and side were trying to overload his pain receptors.

After taking a few deep breaths, he stood and walked as quietly as he could toward the bookshelf. He scanned the backs of a few of the books before settling on one of the thrillers. By the time he made it back to the bed, he was reconsidering the pain-pill-avoidance thing. But all he had to do was think about his parents, and the urge to ever pop anything stronger than an aspirin in his mouth dissolved.

He lay back with the book and tried to read, but his mind kept wandering to Chloe. Every time he scanned her bedroom, he spotted something that revealed a little more of who she was. Her nightstand held a photo of her with her brothers when they were younger, all astride horses and dressed as you'd expect ranch kids to be dressed. A trophy sat atop a filing cabinet, probably for something like best grade point average in a high school science class. One of those picture frames that held several snapshots hung above her desk alongside a wildflower calendar.

Even though he knew he should keep his distance as much as he could while staying in her home, he couldn't deny that a part of him wanted to get to know her better. He felt drawn to her, and he was pretty sure it was by more than her witty personality.

At some point he fell asleep only to wake up just as dawn was barely peeking its head above the horizon. He heard movement in the distance and figured it was Chloe walking around the kitchen. Though he was tired, he didn't feel as if he were going to fall back asleep anytime soon. With more than a few grunts and biting down on his lower lip, he got up and slipped on his jeans and shirt. He didn't bother with his boots. They'd just make a bunch of noise anyway.

He eased his way out of the room and down the hallway toward the kitchen. When he caught sight of Chloe, he paused and watched her make coffee. Gone was the professional, put-together look. Rather, she wore a T-shirt and pajama bottoms, her bare toes poking out from beneath the hem. If he'd thought her pretty before, she was downright sexy now, as if she'd just crawled from the bed next to him. If he didn't think he'd be slapped into next week, he'd be willing to risk some pain from his injuries to press her against the kitchen counter and kiss her breathless.

That image caused his jeans to grow uncomfortable. When he attempted to shift to a less abrasive position, she gasped. She raised her hand to her heart.

"Scare a girl to death, won't you?"

"Sorry. Didn't mean to."

A bit of her physician's persona slipped into place. "You're up early. Are you okay?"

"Fine. Sleep cycle is just messed up."

She nodded. "That happens a lot to people who are in the hospital."

He walked slowly into the room and positioned himself behind the island to hide his aroused state. "Have to say your bed is a lot more comfortable."

She glanced at him for a moment before turning toward the coffeepot. He wondered if he'd flustered her again, if in this setting he actually made her nervous.

"I would offer you some coffee, but you need to rest."

"I'd rather have some decent coffee. Haven't had any of that in a while."

She poured two cups. "I usually sit on the front porch and watch the sunrise."

"Sounds good to me, unless you want to be alone."

She inclined her head toward the front of the house. "Let's go then before we miss the show."

As he hurried as best he could to get ahead of her, he wondered when he was going to feel normal again, well enough to resume his life. But as he opened the door for Chloe, he was glad she'd talked him into coming to her house. He still intended to find some way to pay her and her family back, but he was just so dang grateful to be out of the hospital that he let his pride take a backseat for the moment.

When they stepped outside, he heard clicking. When he looked over, two basset hounds were ambling toward them. "Who are these guys?"

"Wyatt, meet Roscoe and Cletus." She glanced up at him with a smile. "We watched a lot of *Dukes of Hazzard* reruns when we were kids. My parents loved that show. Mom had a thing for Bo Duke."

"Your mom, she's gone?"

A sadness invaded Chloe's eyes and she nodded. "She died in a car wreck when I was nine."

"I'm sorry."

"Thanks." She shifted toward a small table flanked by two rocking chairs. After placing the mugs on the table, she held the back of one of the rocking chairs steady for him.

He was so ready to be able to do whatever he wanted on his own again, but he had a sinking feeling that was going to take longer than he'd like.

Once they were both seated and sipping on the good, rich coffee, the world around the house slowly brightened as if Mother Nature were turning up a dimmer switch. Songbirds started chirping nearby, and a blond, short-haired cat darted out from underneath a pickup truck and raced for the barn.

"Must smell a breakfast mouse," Chloe said.

The eastern horizon started shifting from pale blue to a layer of orange and then yellow. It looked like a painting he'd seen on display at a museum in Oklahoma, a place he'd visited while killing time before a rodeo a couple of years ago.

"I see why you like it here," he said. "You've always lived on the ranch?"

"My whole life with the exception of when I was in college and med school."

He wondered what that was like, to be so connected to a place that it was like a part of the family. He nearly laughed at that. With the exception of his grandparents, he'd never really had much of a family. Whenever he'd seen movies with big, traditional families, they'd always seemed odd to him, as unreal as superhero cartoons.

But even though Chloe's mom was gone, he'd seen one of those types of families the night before. And he'd found himself wondering what it'd be like to be more than a temporary guest at their table, a part of something that seemed so strong, so real.

They settled into companionable silence, and he didn't feel the need to fill it. Neither, evidently, did Chloe. As he watched the world wake to a new day, he tried not to think about how intoxicating this little slice of heaven could be, how it was already luring him like a very addictive drug.

Chapter Eight

By lunchtime, Chloe was so frustrated that she had to get away from the clinic for a while. So she grabbed the sandwich she'd brought to work and headed to the park by the lake. She needed the sun and fresh air, and time to not feel so helpless. Sitting on top of a picnic table and staring out across Blue Falls Lake, she tried to tell herself that she couldn't solve everyone's problems, the patient currently staying at her house notwithstanding.

"I thought that was you down here."

Chloe looked up to see Skyler Bradshaw approaching from the walkway that led up to the Wildflower Inn, which Skyler owned. Her friend was so pregnant she looked as if she were going to pop.

"What are you doing toddling down here?"

"Probably same as you. Wanted to get outside and enjoy the pleasant weather for a bit. Feels nice after the rain last night."

"Yeah." Chloe gestured toward Skyler's rounded belly. "How's the wee one doing?"

"Rambunctious. Little guy is definitely his father's child."

Chloe smiled despite a little pang of longing. Damn that ticking clock. "Have you picked out a name?"

"Ethan Lane."

"Sounds like a future rodeo rider to me."

"Lord help me, I'll be a nervous wreck if that happens. But speaking of rodeo riders, the town grapevine is abuzz with the fact that you took Wyatt Kelley home with you."

"Yes, and I'm sure I know where that grapevine started and that Verona already has us married off with two-point-five kids."

Skyler laughed. "You've got her pegged. I hate to admit it, but she does have the touch."

"It's just temporary, only until he's well enough to be on his own again. Then he'll be gone."

"Stranger things have happened. You're talking to the gal whose uncharacteristic one-night stand turned into true love." She shook her head and placed her hand atop her stomach. "I still can't believe it sometimes."

"It was just a kindness of necessity."

"Is he the reason you seemed a million miles away a few minutes ago?"

"No. Well, maybe partially. It's just been one of those days when I wish I could wave a magic wand and make everything better."

"What's wrong?"

Chloe sighed. "Ruth Carter had another heart attack last night and isn't doing very well. Another patient had let his diabetes get so out of control that he's going to lose a foot. And then a teenage girl came in with pneumonia and undiagnosed asthma. When I asked her parents why they hadn't brought her in earlier, they said it was because they were both out of work and didn't have insurance."

"Tough morning."

"Yeah. Sometimes I feel helpless, as if what I do doesn't make a dent, not for the people who really need it."

"Are you kidding? You're one of the most caring people I know. Who else would take a near stranger into her home just because he didn't have anywhere else to go? I mean, it doesn't hurt that he's reportedly drop-dead gorgeous."

Chloe rolled her eyes. "You, too?"

Skyler shrugged. "What can I say? Happiness has brought out the sappy side of me."

Chloe smiled at her friend, something that was normally easy to do. But now? The edges of her mouth felt heavy as she tugged them upward. She had to shake off the melancholy. Feeling down wasn't like her at all, and she didn't like it. Besides, she had too much to do to allow a little case of the blues to mess with her.

Chloe slid off the table and brushed at the back of her slacks. "I better get back to work. Let me give you a ride up to the inn."

Skyler waved away the offer. "Maybe if I hoof it up the hill, this baby will decide to make an appearance."

"As your doctor, I say he needs a few more days in the oven."

"Said like someone who doesn't know how miserable this is."

Not so long ago, Chloe would have simply laughed at that comment. But today it stung, and she couldn't muster a laugh, only a small smile that she hoped would suffice.

Chloe drove back to the clinic but didn't immediately get out of her car. She needed to force an attitude adjustment before she went in to greet her next patient.

But despite her best efforts to be positive, her afternoon lineup didn't help bolster her mood. It seemed this was the day for seeing people who needed more help than she could give. By the time she headed for home, she was worn out. And her day never stopped when she left work. She just traded one set of tasks for another.

She didn't mind, really. After all, she loved her dad and brothers. Though they might rarely say it out loud, that love had strengthened after her mom died. She was thankful for every day she had with them.

But when did she get to have time that was hers alone?

Where had that come from? She did not want to tempt fate by letting those kinds of thoughts take up residence. She had a good life and no right to complain. As she'd seen today, there were a lot of people much worse off than her.

Her thoughts were so wrapped up in the patients she'd seen throughout the day that she couldn't believe she'd forgotten she had yet another at home. When she pulled up in front of the house, he was sitting on the front porch scratching Roscoe's head. She smiled and felt some of the stress of the day slip from her shoulders. It was good to be home.

"Looks as if you've made a new friend," she said as she got out of her car.

"I have a feeling these two like whoever feeds them."

Chloe glanced at the dog bowls as she climbed the front steps and saw that they'd been filled. "You didn't have to do that."

"Not like it was hard work."

Though she needed to go in and start dinner, she

plopped down into the chair next to Wyatt's. "So, what else did you do today?"

"Nothing strenuous, if that's what you're worried about. Read some, slept some, had long, one-sided conversations with the dogs. How was your day?"

She was on the verge of saying "fine" when she found herself spilling the details of her frustrating day. When she was done, she glanced over at him. "Sorry you asked?"

"No."

She could tell he meant it, and the first genuine smile of the day lifted the edges of her lips. "Thanks for listening."

He shrugged. "Not like I'm going to get up and run away."

She laughed. "True. I wonder why I never thought of this captive-audience thing before." She looked out toward the barn, waved at Emmett as he left for the day. "I just wish everyone listened to what I said as much as you did."

"I'm not the poster child for good patients."

She glanced over at him, realizing that after only one full day at the ranch he'd gained back more color than he had the entire time he'd been in the hospital. "You are a little on the stubborn side, I'll give you that. But some people, well, the decisions they make are sometimes out of ignorance. Others, pure stupidity."

"You can't make people do what they don't want to."

She knew that, but it still didn't sit well with her. She believed that all problems had solutions if you could just pinpoint them.

But the solution to the medical problems of Blue Falls would have to wait. Right now, the problem of no dinner being prepared was next on her list. At least that was a problem she could fix.

WYATT DIDN'T LIKE the way fatigue and worry about her patients were weighing Chloe down. When he'd met her at the hospital, she'd seemed so chipper. But he supposed even the happiest person had problems.

She stood, though she looked as if she'd rather do anything else. "I'll swap out your bandages after I get dinner started."

"I already did it."

"Oh. Did you carefully clean and dry the incisions well before you put on new bandages?"

"Yes."

"Check for infection?"

"Yes, Doc. I did everything exactly how you did it yesterday. Stop worrying."

"It's my job."

"You're not at work anymore." Was she ever in "off" mode?

He'd ask her if she needed help with dinner, but he knew she'd say no. Plus, he wasn't exactly a whiz in the kitchen. Still, he waited a few seconds after she went inside then followed her. He reached the living room in time to hear her laugh.

Chloe stood next to the small table at the edge of the room that was flanked by two ladder-back chairs. She pointed at the Scrabble board he'd set up after spotting the game in a well-worn box on the bookcase in the corner.

"You remembered how the board was on the game we didn't get to finish."

"I wasn't going to miss my opportunity to win."

"Ha." She grabbed the bag of tiles and drew out enough for her next turn. After a bit of rearranging and obvious mental calculating of scores, she played her word. She glanced at him with a satisfied grin before heading into the kitchen.

With a smile tugging at his mouth, he slowly made his way across the living room and looked down at the word and where she'd written her score. Damn if she didn't get thirty-two points out of it.

"We should make this game more interesting with a wager," he called out.

She popped her head around the corner. "I wouldn't be that confident you're going to win."

"Too scared to bet that you will?"

She lifted an eyebrow. "What were you thinking?"

"I'm not sure yet. But I'll come up with something good."

"I can hardly wait." Then she disappeared back into the kitchen.

He chose his own tiles and played the only word he could come up with for a measly three points. Maybe he shouldn't bet anything big after all.

By the time he walked into the kitchen, she had thick, juicy burgers frying atop the stove and had pulled a potato salad out of the fridge. He had no idea when she'd had time to make that.

"So, Dr. Chloe Brody, what made a girl who grew up on a cattle ranch want to become a doctor? Vet might have made more sense."

She paused in her movements for a couple of moments before flipping the burgers. She still didn't answer for a few more beats. "My mom used to work at the hospital when I was a kid. She was a nurse's aide.

I used to hang out with her. I was always amazed that these people in white coats knew what was wrong with a person and how to make it better."

He had the oddest sense there was more behind her reason, but he didn't push. He didn't know her well enough to push. They were doctor and patient, nothing more. Although the more time he spent with her, the more he thought about what it might be like to move on to being friends, perhaps more than friends.

At that moment, the back door opening announced the arrival of her family. As if kicked out of a day-dream, Chloe moved to the cabinet and pulled out plates. Without asking, he stepped to the drawer next to the sink and pulled out silverware.

"Oh, honey, I meant to call you earlier and tell you we wouldn't need dinner tonight," her dad said when he entered the room. "Simon is having a meeting in town tonight with the ranchers in the area about the vandals. Your brothers and I are going. We'll grab a bite in town."

"Okay." Chloe sounded as if she didn't mind having gone to the effort of cooking for no reason.

The thing was, Wyatt did mind. He might barely know her, and her dad and brothers seemed nice enough, but what little he'd seen didn't seem fair to him. Sure, the Brody men worked hard on the ranch all day, but Chloe worked long hours, too. And then she came home and did all the cooking and cleaning, who knew what else.

But he was the stranger imposing on their hospital-ity. What could he say that wouldn't be rude?

"You know, I'm pretty hungry today," Wyatt said.

"I could probably polish off two or three of those burgers myself."

Chloe met his gaze and smiled such a sweet, grateful smile that he knew if he didn't get out of this house soon he wasn't going to be able to keep his hands off her. And he wasn't the kind of man she needed in her life. He was nothing more than a wanderer, a man who barely made ends meet most of the time, someone who started running from his past the moment he could and hadn't stopped since. She was smart, beautiful, rooted in this land and deserved someone a lot better than him. Someone who could give her whatever she wanted.

Still, while he was her guest, he could be friendly and help in whatever small ways he could.

By the time the burgers were done, he and Chloe were the only people left on the ranch. He winced as he sat.

Chloe slid into the chair opposite him, where Owen had sat the night before. "Hurting?"

"A little. Nothing I can't handle." With a lot of mental cursing.

Chloe started to stand again. "I'll get you another pain pill."

Without thinking, he grabbed her hand to stop her. She froze and met his gaze.

He liked the feel of her soft hand beneath his, so much so that he didn't immediately release her. "I'm okay."

Chloe didn't pull away, but common sense had him releasing her.

"There's no sense in you hurting when you don't have to," she said.

"I've seen guys who've been injured get hooked

on painkillers. I don't want to risk it." That wasn't the main reason, but he would never know Chloe well enough to divulge the secret he shared with no one.

Chloe exhaled slowly but slid fully back into her seat. The fact that she wasn't arguing the point further told him how tired she was after her long day.

Despite his earlier comment that he could down two or three burgers, he had only managed one and a single scoop of the potato salad. It had nothing to do with the taste or his hunger but rather the fact that sitting in the hard chair was making his injuries hurt even more. Even so, he couldn't make himself go to bed. He'd lain on his back so much lately that he was getting tired of looking at ceilings. The next time he spent that much time in bed, he hoped he was having a lot more fun.

An image of Chloe beneath the sheets with him slapped him right in an area that made it necessary to stay seated at the table while Chloe put away the leftovers and placed the dirty dishes in the dishwasher.

"Want to watch TV?" she asked when she was done.

"Sure." Thankfully, his sudden erection had calmed down enough that he could stand.

By the time he reached the couch, he dreaded the act of sitting down again. The up and down always caused the worst pain. Chloe must have picked up on his hesitation because she positioned herself in front of him and extended her hands.

"What are you doing?"

"Grab my hands. I'll help you ease down."

"I can sit on my own."

"Oh, do stop arguing with me."

He smiled at her exasperation. "Yes, ma'am."

Though she did her best to help him, his stomach still felt as if he were being cut with a machete.

"I know it doesn't seem like it, but it should start causing less pain soon."

"Good." He was looking forward to not wanting to curse a blue streak every time he sat down.

Chloe sank onto the other end of the couch and kicked off her shoes. She stretched her toes upward as she leaned her arms against her knees. She looked dog-tired.

When she lifted one foot to massage it, he knew how he could repay her in a small way. He patted the couch next to him. "Lay back and prop your feet up here."

She glanced over at him. "What?"

"I'll give you a foot rub."

"Uh, no. My feet have been stuck in these shoes all day."

He chuckled at how she thought that might matter. "You do realize I'm around cowboys and livestock all the time, right? I don't think your feet are going to bother me."

"Wyatt—"

"Feet, now, or do you want me to risk injury by bending over and grabbing them?"

She sighed in defeat and spun so that her feet were next to his thigh.

As he propped her feet on top of his leg, she tensed. "Are you ticklish?"

"No."

"Then relax."

"That's hard to do when a stranger has your feet."

He met her gaze and smiled. "I think we're past the

stranger stage, don't you? I mean, you have seen me without my shirt."

"I've seen lots of guys without their shirts. Doesn't mean we're friends."

"But do you play Scrabble with them? Kidnap them and keep them in your home?"

Her mouth dropped open. "I did not kidnap you."

He chuckled at how easily he'd gotten an indignant reaction out of her.

"Oh, you." She grabbed a decorative pillow and swatted his arm with it.

"Don't hit the injured guy."

Instead of responding, she simply rolled her eyes and leaned her head back against the arm of the couch.

Wyatt used his thumbs to work the balls of her feet. She stayed tense for a few moments more before beginning to relax. He glanced over right before she closed her eyes. He smiled, glad he was able to finally do something to repay her in the tiniest way. He shifted his focus to her feet and noticed that her toenails were painted a pale blue, and each of her big toes sported a white daisy. Even though her feet were covered up most of the time, she still wanted cute toes.

He worked his way slowly from the balls of her feet to the arches, and a sound of appreciation escaped Chloe. Damn if it didn't make Wyatt go hard. He decided to pretend it wasn't happening so hopefully Chloe wouldn't notice. Her having this effect on him was getting damned inconvenient. If he didn't cut it out, he was going to get caught.

"I'm going to need to call my friend Linnea in Dallas tomorrow and tell her she's lost her best-friend status," she said without opening her eyes.

"Like it, huh?"

"It feels awesome, so much better than when I rub my own feet. You should give up rodeo and become a foot masseur."

He snorted at that. "Your feet are one thing. I don't want to rub some dude's feet."

She smiled at that, and this time something moved in his chest.

Oh, hell no. He couldn't feel anything for Chloe, nothing beyond some casual flirtation. A good foot massage was about the best thing he could offer her. And yet he couldn't keep his mind from wandering, from imagining what it might be like if he were the kind of guy who could stay in one place and have a normal job. If he were from a normal family and could give Chloe even a fraction of what she deserved.

Maybe the massage was a bad idea. He paused and glanced over at Chloe. All his doubts faded away, at least for the moment, when he saw that she had fallen asleep. Though it made him yearn for things that could never be, he didn't regret helping her relax after a long day. He could live with the sting of loneliness he suspected he'd feel when he left Blue Falls. After all, it wouldn't be the first time. He and that empty feeling were old acquaintances.

But as he watched Chloe sleep, something he couldn't quite identify shifted inside him and he knew with an absolute certainty that this time it was different. This time, it was going to do a bit more than sting.

Chapter Nine

Chloe didn't want to wake up, not when she felt so good, so relaxed. But she could feel herself drifting upward toward the surface despite her efforts to prevent it. A sudden loud noise followed quickly by laughter yanked her the rest of the way out of sleep and caused her to jump.

A cry confused her for a moment as she looked away from where her family was standing inside the front door toward the agonized sound. In a horrible flash, she realized what had happened. She'd accidentally kicked Wyatt in the stomach, and his entire body was clenched taut with pain.

"Oh, my God," she said as she slipped her feet to the floor and closed the distance between them. "I'm so sorry, Wyatt."

He didn't respond, probably because he was fighting not to let the tears pooled in his eyes break free.

"I need you to lie down so I can check your wounds."

He didn't move, so she looked at Owen, who she realized had been the one laughing. She ignored the why for the moment.

"Help me."

Owen jumped into action, not needing further instructions. He shifted Wyatt's legs to the couch while Chloe held one hand gently against Wyatt's stomach and eased his head to the opposite couch arm from the one she'd been using to prop her pillow.

Wyatt clenched his teeth and moaned again. She hadn't heard him give voice to that much pain since the night he'd been brought into the ER with fresh lacerations. When he was finally stretched along the length of the couch, she edged his hand away from his middle and lifted his shirt. The muscle in his jaw tightened as she carefully peeled back the bandage along the lower part of his abdomen.

She let out a slow breath of relief when she saw that all the stitches were intact and that there was no visible blood.

"I know that this is a dumb question, but how does it feel?"

"Swell," Wyatt said, his voice strained.

"Everything looks fine, but after this initial pain passes I want you to tell me if anything feels different, okay?"

He nodded once, just a slight motion but enough to let her know that he heard her.

She took his hand and squeezed it. "I'm really sorry. I didn't mean to hurt you."

"I know."

"It's my fault," Owen said from where he sat on the edge of the adjacent chair. "Sorry, man."

Chloe looked at her brother and saw genuine regret there. "Go to my room and get one of his pain pills."

"No," Wyatt said, shaking his head.

"Yes." She was firm, leaving no room for argument. When her gaze met his, she saw his desire to rebel.

Thankfully, he didn't, either because he didn't want to argue in front of her family or because he really did need the pain medicine no matter how much he wanted to avoid taking it.

Without looking at her brothers or dad, she went to the kitchen to get a glass of water, arriving back in the living room at the same time as Owen. She handed Wyatt the pain pill and for a moment he simply stared at it before popping it into his mouth. When he lifted his head, she held the glass to his lips. He swallowed then nodded, and she set the water on the coffee table.

After a moment, Wyatt took a deeper breath.

"Are you okay?" she asked.

"Well, I don't recommend getting kicked in the stomach, but I'll live."

Chloe slid onto the coffee table and relaxed a little. Only then did she shift her gaze to her brothers and dad. "How'd the meeting go?" Best to move to a topic far from why she'd had her feet on Wyatt's lap in the first place.

"Frustrating," her dad said as he dropped into his usual chair. "Nobody's gotten a good look at these bastards, and their movements seem random."

Garrett leaned against his dad's chair. "Simon is at a loss where to place a stakeout to try to catch them in the act."

"Maybe you need to set up a sort of neighborhood watch among the ranchers," Wyatt said. "Several years ago, there was a string of cattle thefts up in Wyoming. The ranchers banded together and set up watches at all the ranches. They kept it quiet so the thieves wouldn't get wind of it, and they caught them within a week."

"Not a bad idea," her dad said. "Lot of ground to cover, but we can try."

"I'll talk to Simon tomorrow," Garrett said.

They all chatted a few minutes more before her brothers and dad headed to bed.

Chloe looked at where Wyatt was still lying on the couch, his forearm propped against his forehead. "You think you can make it to bed, or do you need to rest a little longer?"

"I think I'll just sleep here tonight."

"You'd be more comfortable in the bed."

Wyatt looked at her. "I have slept in way less comfortable places. Don't worry so much. I'm fine."

"At least as fine as you can be after your doctor kicked you in the stomach."

"Hey, what are friends for?"

She smiled at that. "That's one lousy friend."

"Nah. I'd say you're a pretty good one."

Something about the way he said those words, combined with the sincerity she saw in his eyes, touched her so deeply that she had to look away. She felt him suddenly become more important, in danger of carving out a little piece of her heart for himself. And she couldn't allow that. They could be friends, nothing more.

"You okay?" he asked.

"Yeah, just tired. If you're sure you'll be okay here, I'm going to head to bed. Do you need anything from the bedroom? Pajamas?"

He smiled. "I don't own pajamas."

Heat rushed up her neck into her face at the image that popped into her head. Somehow she doubted he'd been sleeping in his shirt and jeans.

Needing to put some distance between them, she said good-night and forced herself to walk normally to her room. But when she slipped inside the bedroom and closed the door behind her, she leaned against it and closed her eyes, took a deep breath. Wyatt Kelley needed to get well and be on his way before she started having the wrong sorts of thoughts about him, the ones that came to mind when she imagined him sleeping in her bed wearing next to nothing. Or maybe nothing at all.

Her face heated even more at that mental picture. It'd been a long time since she'd been with a man, but being that way with Wyatt was exactly where her thoughts went. Crazy, absolutely crazy. Though they weren't total strangers anymore, she certainly didn't know him well enough to be thinking about having sex with him.

Well, why not? She'd had fantasies about actors in movies. Why was that any different than a sexy cowboy she barely knew?

Because that sexy cowboy was in the next room and making her like him more every day.

WYATT DIDN'T WANT to move ever again, but his bladder had different ideas. So he gritted his teeth and forced himself to a sitting position. By the time he managed that, he was pretty sure he deserved some sort of reward for not screaming. The pain pill had allowed him to rest, but it was long gone. Now he faced a day of having to resist taking another one. He'd flush them all if he didn't think Chloe would notice.

By the time he'd made it halfway down the hall to the bathroom, he was pretty sure he was hurting as much as he had the night the bull had tried to do him in. Still, when he thought of how Chloe had felt relaxed enough to sleep with her feet propped on his leg, he had to smile.

When he exited the bathroom a few minutes and a few silent curses later, Chloe was standing in the hall waiting for him.

"How do you feel this morning?"

"Okay."

"You're lying."

"Yep, I am," he said as he made his way past her toward the living room. At the end of the hall, he changed directions and walked into the kitchen.

Chloe followed him, as he'd known she would. "Let me check your wounds."

"They're fine. I looked while I was in the bathroom." She didn't need to know there was now a bruise around one end of his incision. It would just make her feel worse about what had happened.

"I'd ask if you want another pain pill, but I already know the answer to that." She crossed to the counter and started a pot of coffee.

"Smart woman."

She opened the refrigerator. "Any special requests for dinner tonight?"

"No, and you don't have to cook for me."

"I told you—"

"I know what you said. Why doesn't anyone else cook or clean but you?"

"They're all busy, away from the house all day."

"So are you."

She closed the fridge and grabbed a bagel instead.

After she popped it in the toaster, she turned and leaned back against the counter. "Old habits."

Something about the faraway look in her eyes told him a story more than words. "You've been doing this since your mother passed, haven't you?"

She was quiet so long that he thought she might not answer. But finally her gaze fixed on his.

"Yeah." She sounded surprised, as if somehow she hadn't realized what she'd been doing for all those years.

She looked so alone in that moment that Wyatt wanted to pull her into his arms. If he'd been standing close to her, he probably would have.

"You were only a kid."

"So were my brothers, and my dad..." Her voice faltered and she looked down at the floor. "His heart broke so much that he could barely function for a while. If not for Garrett, Owen and me, I wonder if he might have never bounced back." She shifted her weight from one foot to the other and glanced at him. "They really loved each other, that kind of love that only happens once."

"That's why he never remarried?"

She nodded. "He doesn't ever talk about it, but I know he still mourns Mom. He puts fresh flowers on her grave every week."

An unfamiliar lump rose in Wyatt's throat. He had no idea what that kind of love looked like. His grandparents had had a good marriage, but he'd never gotten the sense it was that epic, fairy-tale type of love that he wasn't sure really existed in the real world. Except here Chloe was telling him that she'd seen it with her own eyes with her parents.

It was a good thing he'd be leaving soon, before he got too close. Even if he were a different kind of man from a different family, how could he live up to what she likely expected in a man after she'd seen the kind of love her father had felt for her mother?

He couldn't.

"I better get ready for work," she said. "Do you need anything before I go?"

"I'm fine, Chloe. Don't worry about me."

She stood and watched him for a moment. "I don't think I know how to stop."

As she walked out of the room, he wished there were some way he could alleviate the weight she seemed to carry. But she was so different from him, worrying about and caring for everyone around her— family, friends, patients—while he kept his distance from people. It was just easier that way. If you didn't care, they couldn't hurt you.

CHLOE THREW HERSELF into work the moment she got to the clinic, but no matter how many patients she saw she couldn't shake the feeling that something had shifted in her that morning. It wasn't as if she were unaware of how much she did for her brothers and father, but she never actively thought about it.

But in the aftermath of her mother's death, Chloe had seen the need for someone to fill her mother's shoes. Even at nine years old, she'd known that person should be her. It wasn't even that she was the only girl and thus should do the "girl" things like cooking and cleaning. It was that she'd known she would be better at them than her dad and brothers. And now that she thought about it with more than twenty years' worth of distance, maybe some part of her had jumped into that role to deal with her own sorrow and never let go of it for fear the grief would swallow her whole. It had taken a few simple words from someone who'd just come into her life to make her see that.

She wasn't sure if she was thankful or resented Wyatt for showing her the truth.

After lunch she went to do her rounds at the hospital. When she reached Ruth Carter's room, the older woman looked so pale and thin, even more so than when Wyatt had been a patient a few doors down. The fact that Ruth was watching TV instead of knitting told Chloe how very tired the older woman was. Still, Ruth managed a small smile when she saw her.

"Hey, there." Chloe glanced up at the TV. "Anything good on today?"

"Nope, but hope springs eternal."

Chloe smiled at that as she checked over Ruth's chart.

"How's your friend doing?" Ruth asked.

"Which friend is that?"

"The good-looking one who likes to flirt."

"Oh, Wyatt. He's just a patient."

Ruth made a dismissive sound. "Now, honey, I know your mama taught you not to lie. I saw how you looked at that boy."

"Oh, really? And how was that?" Chloe moved to the side of the bed to check Ruth's pulse.

"Like you could gobble him up."

"Ruth, dear, I think you're imagining things."

"I might be old and my time getting shorter, but I can still see plenty fine. And I saw he was looking at you the same way."

Chloe leaned her hip against the edge of the bed and narrowed her eyes. "Have you been talking to Verona Charles?"

Ruth laughed a little. "No, but you asking me that means I'm not the only one who's seen the spark between you and Wyatt. You would make cute babies."

That idea sent a shock wave through Chloe, followed by a flood of images—her in Wyatt's arms, him kissing her, them making love, her holding a baby and Wyatt looking down at the little face with love in his eyes. The rush of longing that grabbed hold of her stole her breath, and it was all she could do to fake being okay until she was out of Ruth's room. Luckily, Ruth was her last patient, so Chloe hurried outside, needing great gulps of fresh air.

What was wrong with her? It felt as if she'd been holding up walls around her and they'd all come caving in, swamping her with a flood of emotions.

How could she have such feelings for Wyatt when he'd only come into her life such a short time ago? Why him? Why a guy she couldn't have? Even if she could, was she strong enough to put herself in the position of experiencing a loss like her father had endured? Was taking that kind of chance worth it?

All of those questions plagued her through the rest of the day, but as she headed home she still didn't have any answers. Needing more time to think, she drove over to the Mehlerhaus Bakery and bought some cookies to take home. While waiting to pay for them, she watched as Keri Teague, the owner of the bakery, handed a newly baked birthday cake over to Talia Monroe.

"Tell Jake I said, 'Happy birthday,'" Keri said.

"I will. Thanks." Talia turned to leave. "Oh, hey, Chloe. I didn't see you. How are you doing?"

"Fine, thanks."

"Sorry to run, but I've got to pick up Mia."

Chloe watched as Talia hurried out the door to retrieve her stepdaughter. That longing Chloe had been experiencing lately came to the fore again. Talia and Jake Monroe were yet another couple that Verona had steered toward each other with happily-ever-after results. Part of Chloe wanted to stop fighting her attraction to Wyatt and just see what happened, but another part was downright scared of the same thing.

"Can I help you, Chloe?"

She jerked her attention away from the now empty doorway. "Uh, yeah." She pointed at the display case. "A dozen of the molasses cookies, please."

"Your guest have a sweet tooth?"

"I don't know, but I do."

Keri laughed at that. "Good. I love people with a sweet tooth. It keeps me in business."

As Keri put the cookies in a box, Chloe's thoughts drifted back to the birthday cake and realization hit. Her dad's sixtieth birthday was right around the corner. Sixty. Wow, that was hard to believe. And to her way of thinking, it deserved a big party.

"I also need to order a birthday cake."

After placing the order for the cake, she headed home with plans for her dad's surprise party swirling in her head.

When she stepped through the front door a few minutes later, she halted in her tracks. From the sound of the banging in the kitchen and the scent of frying grease, someone was cooking. Thinking she'd walked into an alternate universe, she crossed the living room. At the entrance to the kitchen, she stopped again and stared. Wyatt was standing at the stove, muttering to himself.

"What are you doing?"

He glanced over his shoulder. "Hey. I'm cooking dinner."

"You shouldn't be doing that, especially not after what happened last night."

"I'm fine."

She took a few steps into the room and slid the box of cookies onto the table. "If this is some sort of effort to pay for your keep, it's not necessary."

"If you want me to stay here, you're going to have to deal with me trying to help out."

"But you need to rest to get better."

"I rest plenty, so much I'm going to go crazy if I can't do something beside lie around or sit on the porch."

She shook her head. "Fine, at long as you don't overdo it. Here, I can help you."

He held out a spatula. "No, I've got it covered." He used the spatula to make a shooing motion. "Go take a nap or a bubble bath, whatever girls do to relax."

She started to laugh at the idea of indulging in a bubble bath when she could be doing something productive. But she thought about what he'd said that morning, that she was always taking care of everyone else, living the role she'd assigned herself when she was still in elementary school. So she stopped herself from mentally writing a to-do list that she could tick off before dinner.

Why not take a bubble bath? She'd worked hard

all day. She deserved a little time to relax. And if it made her smell pretty and Wyatt liked it? Well, that sounded okay, too.

"Okay, I think I will. Thank you."

He smiled and nodded, and her heart did a little flip. Even when he turned back to the stove, she stared at him a few moments longer. When was the last time anyone had cooked for her? Before she stalked across the room and pulled his mouth to hers, she forced herself down the hallway.

The moment she sank into the bath a few minutes later, she felt the stress of the day start to drift away. She closed her eyes and laid her head against the end of the tub. She couldn't remember the last time she'd been this relaxed, and she had Wyatt to thank for it.

She let her thoughts drift to what Ruth had said about a spark. Was there something between her and Wyatt against all the odds that would say otherwise? And even if a spark did exist, did it make any sense to explore it when Wyatt would leave as soon as he was able? Considering he was standing in her kitchen cooking dinner, that day might be sooner rather than later.

Her heart squeezed at that thought, and she realized she'd miss him when he was gone. It was best not to get too attached, to keep her distance, to guard her heart.

Her eyes popped open at that last thought. Had she been doing that her whole life? Was that why every relationship she'd ever had hadn't lasted more than a handful of months? Had losing her mother so young broken something inside her, making her unable to commit, unable to fully give herself to another person and accept him in return?

She thought of all the years her father had been

alone, how Garrett still wasn't married, how Owen flitted from one woman to the next. Maybe they were all broken and didn't realize it.

Chapter Ten

Chloe reached the end of the hallway just as Owen asked, "Why does it smell like flowers in here?"

"Because I took a bath." She thumped the front of his hat, nearly tipping it off his head, as she walked past him toward the kitchen. "You should try it sometime."

"I bathe. Just not going to come out smelling like flowers. You got a hot date or something?"

She ignored him, but he followed her as Garrett and her dad filed in behind him.

"And if you're going out, who's cooking dinner?"

She stopped and turned back toward him, causing Owen to pull up short and the others to almost run into the back of him. "I'm not going out, but even if I was it wouldn't hurt you to slap together a sandwich."

When she spun and continued into the kitchen, she heard Owen mutter, "What's gotten into her?"

Chloe entered the kitchen in time to see Wyatt scraping hard to get something out of a skillet. Okay, that didn't look promising. Still, she'd give him the benefit of the doubt. He was trying to help even though she would be happier if he took it easy. She supposed that might be too much to ask for, however.

"Um, you put the hurt guy to work?"

Wyatt looked at Owen. "No, I volunteered. Earn my keep."

"That wasn't necessary, son."

Something about how her dad called Wyatt "son" made Chloe feel as if Wyatt had shifted a little more firmly into the picture she was getting used to seeing in her family kitchen. It was strange, and dangerous, how easily that had happened. If she knew what was good in the long run, for all of them, she'd make a stronger effort to keep her distance.

"I'm not one for sitting around doing nothing and not paying my own way."

Her dad nodded once in understanding because he was much the same. It hit Chloe just how much they were alike—hardworking, self-sufficient and with a good dose of stubbornness thrown in.

As her dad and brothers washed their hands in the kitchen sink, Chloe moved to help Wyatt, only to have him wave her toward the table. Not wanting to dispel her good mood from the bath by arguing, she took her seat, followed quickly by the rest of her family.

When Wyatt put a bowl of what appeared to be mashed potatoes on the table, Chloe bit down on a twinge of worry. It looked as if Wyatt had done battle with the potatoes and they'd won. But looks didn't always matter with food. It was the taste that counted. Next came a bowl of beets he'd gotten from one of the cans in the pantry. Finally, he placed a plate of fried chicken on the table. She spotted a few charred spots, but she pretended as though she didn't see them.

With all the food now on the table, Wyatt slid onto his chair. Chloe could tell he was wiped out, that he'd probably done too much. Damn fool man.

They started passing around the food, and she realized just how hungry she was. The moment she cut into the chicken, however, she knew it wasn't going to be edible. While it was blackened in spots on the outside, the meat was nearly raw inside. She eased her fork and knife to the sides of her plate, trying to figure out how to tell everyone not to eat the chicken without hurting Wyatt's feelings. He'd worked so hard, when he should have been resting, only to come up with something that was inedible.

But there was no need for her to say anything. A glance around the table at her brothers' faces told her that the side dishes weren't much better. They all seemed frozen and at a loss for words until Wyatt raised a napkin to his mouth and spit out his food. He stared at the plate for a moment.

"Well, I don't think I have a future as a cook."

All at once, her brothers and dad started laughing. Chloe was horrified until she saw that Wyatt was laughing, too. The moment his gaze met hers, the reins she had on her own laughter slipped.

"It's the thought that counts," she said.

"Unless the thought was to give us all salmonella," Owen said.

That set them all off again, laughing like hyenas. When they all managed to pull themselves under control, her dad placed his napkin atop his nearly untouched meal.

"I think this calls for a trip to Gia's for some pizza."

"You all go on," Chloe said. "Just bring us some back. Wyatt's already done too much today."

"I don't think sitting in a restaurant is going to be any more strenuous than sitting here," Wyatt said.

Why did she even bother? One of these mornings she was going to wake up to find he'd hoofed it into town for his truck and taken off for parts unknown.

Within five minutes, they were piled into two vehicles and headed into Blue Falls for dinner. Her dad and brothers took her dad's twin cab pickup while she drove her car with Wyatt as a passenger just in case he started feeling bad and she needed to get him home.

Home. That, too, had felt natural to think, that her home was also Wyatt's. But it wasn't, never would be. After he left, she needed to explore dating more. That or bury herself in so much work that she filled that pesky emptiness that had been plaguing her.

When they all walked into Gia's a few minutes later, every eye in the place turned toward them. They took the first table they came to that had enough chairs. Though he could have chosen any of them, Wyatt slipped into the chair next to hers. Chloe thought she caught a couple of knowing smiles from people at the neighboring tables.

"Hey, Chloe," India Parrish said as she walked over and slid into the empty chair at the end of the table. "I was going to call you tomorrow, but I hope you don't mind me catching you for a minute now."

"Not at all. What's up?"

India glanced past Chloe, and Chloe realized that her friend didn't know Wyatt. "Oh, this is Wyatt Kelley. He's been healing at our house after his accident at the rodeo."

"I heard. Glad to see you're doing better."

"Thank you," Wyatt said.

Chloe looked over at Wyatt for a moment, and the five o'clock shadow on his cheek made her want to rub her hand along his jaw. She was losing her mind. "Um, Wyatt, this is India Parrish. You know her husband, Liam, who organizes the charity rodeos here."

Wyatt nodded at India. "Nice event, except for that whole little misunderstanding with the bull."

"Don't remind me," she said. "I live in fear of someone getting hurt beyond repair, though the rodeos are bringing in tourists and giving us the means to help a lot of people. Which is what I wanted to talk to you about, Chloe. Liam, Logan and I were talking today about who the next beneficiary should be, so we're asking around for suggestions. I thought maybe you'd seen someone at the clinic or the hospital who might be in need of some assistance."

Chloe thought of the young girl without insurance, along with at least a dozen other people who could use some help. "There's always so many, it's hard to choose one."

"Why not help a bunch at the same time?" Wyatt asked.

Chloe shifted her attention to him. "But how do you choose who to help and who gets left out?"

"Maybe you don't have to. I rode in a rodeo in South Dakota once where they had a health fair set up in conjunction with the regular rodeo events, doing free screenings and the like."

"That's not a bad idea," India said. Then her eyes really lit up. "We could use the funds for a community services day—the health screenings, vision tests, and the community closet at the church could give out clothing, shoes, furniture, whatever people need."

"We could donate some beef, get other ranchers to do the same and have a big barbecue dinner," Chloe's dad said. "A free meal will get people to come. Hold it the same day of the next rodeo and draw even more."

When India looked at the calendar on her phone and tossed out the date, Chloe realized the conflict. "That's not going to work."

"If it's because you've got something up your sleeve for my birthday, then I'd rather you did this," her dad said.

In that moment, Chloe realized that some of her mother's generosity lived on in her dad.

"We could make this an annual event," India said.

"You could…" Wyatt trailed off, not finishing his sentence.

Chloe looked over at him. "What?"

"Pardon me if I'm stepping out of line here, but what if you named the event after your mom? You said she really cared about people when she worked at the hospital."

A lump formed in Chloe's throat, but it wasn't just because the mention of her mother made her miss her anew. That Wyatt would have made such a suggestion after only knowing Chloe and her family for a few days touched her deep in her heart. She found herself without words to respond.

"I think that's an excellent idea," her dad said, filling the silence. "Karen would love something like this, even if she would've been embarrassed to have her name attached to it."

"Great!" India patted Chloe on the arm, drawing her attention away from Wyatt. "We'll talk more about this later. Let me know when you're available for lunch this week."

Chloe nodded.

"Well, I'll let you all eat in peace now." India stood and headed out the door, her pizza box in hand.

They all sat in several moments of awkward silence before the waitress came to take their order.

When they returned to the house more than an hour later, Wyatt predictably looked drained. Even so, he hung around the living room until her dad and Garrett had gone off to bed and Owen had left for his turn at watching for the fence vandals.

"I didn't open my mouth when I shouldn't have, did I?" he asked.

She turned from where she was unnecessarily straightening a pile of magazines on the table next to her dad's chair. "About the health fair? Not at all. It was a great idea."

Wyatt took a couple of steps toward her, and she fought the urge to retreat.

"And when I mentioned naming it after your mom? I'm sorry if I was out of line."

"No. Like Dad said, that was a good idea, too."

"I didn't know. You looked at me funny when I said it. I thought I'd stepped in it."

"I... You just surprised me, that's all. You think you're not earning your stay here, but you keep coming up with good suggestions. First the ranch watch, now this."

He laughed a little at that. "Never been accused of being a think tank before."

She smiled a little. "First time for everything."

"Yeah, I guess." He said it slowly, at the last moment looking at her lips before lifting his gaze to her eyes again.

Chloe swallowed hard, doubting she was able to

hide it from him. Before she did something stupid, that she couldn't take back, she broke eye contact and stepped around him.

"I need to check how well your incisions are healing." Though the thought of looking at even that little sliver of skin caused heat to flood her cheeks. At least her back was to him. Without waiting for Wyatt, she headed to her bedroom and pulled fresh bandages from the bag she'd stored there.

When she turned around, Wyatt was almost done unbuttoning his shirt. "What are you doing?"

He paused. "Taking off my shirt."

"You don't have to do that."

"I'm not going to sleep in it." He smiled as he slipped the last two buttons through the holes and shrugged out of the shirt.

Her mouth went dry, and she was probably staring at him as if she'd never seen a half-naked man before.

Still smiling, Wyatt crossed the space between them. "Do I make you nervous, Dr. Brody?"

She licked her lips before she could think how that might look to him. "No, not at all."

He leaned toward her. "I don't believe you."

That was because she was lying through her teeth. Getting through medical school was a breeze compared to how hard it was to keep her hands off his chest. She managed to scrape together enough willpower and common sense to take a step back and point toward the bed.

"Lie down so I can do my job."

"Never heard it called that before."

She swatted him on the arm. "Behave yourself."

"Well, that's no fun."

She had to agree with him there, though she kept that thought to herself.

When he was stretched out along her bed, she forced herself to focus on his injuries, on removing the old bandages, checking the integrity of the stitches and the color of the skin before applying new bandages. She hated the sight of the bruise she'd caused, but thankfully it wasn't bad enough to be concerning. She was about to step away when Wyatt grabbed her hand.

"Thank you."

"It's nothing."

He squeezed her hand gently. "Not for the bandages. For...for caring."

"Just part of the job."

"I don't think that's true," he said. "At least not for all doctors. You're different. You care more for people you barely know than some people do for their own families."

Before she thought about it, she sank onto the side of the bed, still holding his hand. "Your family?"

He seemed startled by her assumption, maybe even by the fact he'd brought the topic up in the first place. "The only family I have left is my grandpa, and he's in a nursing home in Laramie. Got Alzheimer's."

"I'm sorry."

"Thanks." Wyatt stared at the ceiling, as if he could see all the way to Wyoming. "I'd rather go by a bull's horn than to have my mind slowly slip away."

Though she hated the idea of him being killed, she totally understood where he was coming from. She'd seen too many people lose their memories of loved ones, of their entire lives, to various forms of dementia. She couldn't imagine looking at her brothers or dad and not knowing who they were or not being able to remember what memories she had of her mother.

Chloe shifted more toward Wyatt and placed her other hand atop his. "Tell me about him."

He shifted his gaze to her. "You want to hear about my grandpa?"

"Yeah." It didn't take a big leap to know that Wyatt didn't have many people to talk to, probably even fewer with whom to share family memories.

"What do you want to know?"

"Whatever you want to tell me."

Wyatt returned his gaze to the ceiling, and she imagined him sifting through a file drawer of memories. "I spent a lot of time with my grandparents when I was growing up. Grandpa was a team roper back in the day, but that was before my time. I used to like looking through his old photos of his rodeo days, though."

"Guess you come by the rodeo bug naturally, huh?"

"Yeah."

"Were your parents involved in rodeo, too?"

"No," he said a little too quickly. "But even after Grandpa couldn't compete anymore, he couldn't let it go. He became an announcer and would travel all over the West working rodeos. After Grandma retired from teaching, she went along, working as the rodeo secretary. I'd travel with them, so I grew up with rodeo in my veins."

Chloe wondered about his parents, but she got the message that he didn't want to talk about them.

"Is your Grandma still alive?"

"No. She died a few years ago. Grandpa was already losing some of his memories, but after Grandma died it got worse almost overnight. I think he stopped trying to remember because it hurt."

"That's so sad." She realized she was caressing the top of Wyatt's hand with her thumb, but she didn't stop.

"Stuff like that makes you wonder why people pair up at all."

His words hit so close to what she'd thought earlier that she wondered if it were some sort of sign reminding her to not get too close to Wyatt. Still, she found she didn't want to let go of his hand. As illogical as it sounded, that connection felt deeper than it had any reason to, as if she might float off into the darkness of space if she let go.

Wyatt squeezed her hand, drawing her out of her thoughts.

"You better get some sleep," he said.

She wasn't fooled. Fatigue was written as clearly on his face as if someone had taken a black marker and scrawled the word. But she nodded anyway.

"Thanks for trying to make dinner."

"All I did was waste some of your food."

She smiled. "Good entertainment isn't free."

He snorted. "Glad to know I'm so amusing."

Though she didn't want to, she pulled her hands away from Wyatt's. "Good night."

"Good night, Chloe."

Several minutes later as she lay on the couch staring at her own patch of ceiling, she allowed herself to remember the sound of her name on his lips. She'd liked the way it sounded, liked it way too much. So much that part of her would like to hear it for the rest of her days.

WYATT COULDN'T STAY in the house one minute longer. As soon as he saw the mail carrier stop at the mailbox, he headed out the front door and down the driveway. Though the pain in his side and stomach were constant companions, it felt good to get out in the sun and stretch his legs. By the time he reached the end of the driveway, sweat was pouring off him. But he still halfway wanted to keep going, to push himself into Blue Falls. He needed to leave and soon, before he let a scene like what happened in Chloe's bedroom a few nights before lead where he'd wanted it to.

She was a good woman, and she didn't need someone like him dragging all his sordid baggage into her life. Letting her play doc for a few days was one thing. Allowing himself to care for her was another.

Maybe she'd already realized that because since the night he'd told her about his grandpa, since she'd held his hand between hers, she'd made herself scarce, working even longer hours than before. She said it was because they were scrambling like crazy to get everything ready for the health and community fair, but part of him wondered if that were all it was.

He took advantage of her absence and did what the pain allowed to get stronger—climbing the stairs several times a day, using items around the house to lift as makeshift weights, spending time out in the sun and fresh air so the walls would stop closing in on him. His recovery was going slower than he'd like, but at least he could see and feel steady improvement.

He began to look at the rodeo schedule, estimating when he might be able to ride again. He was losing precious time, points and money every day he had to spend in recovery, and he was itching to get back to the sights, sounds and smells of a rodeo arena. But at least he was on a ranch instead of in that awful hospital.

As he turned back toward the house, he spotted

Roscoe and Cletus ambling down the driveway toward him.

"Hey, fellas."

He carefully bent to scratch both of them between the ears. "You two have got it made."

Wyatt winced against a familiar pain as he stood straight. He took a deep breath, wondering how he was going to get on a bull anytime soon if just bending to pet a dog felt as if he might rip himself open again.

Small steps. Small steps. He had to keep reminding himself that small steps would get him where he wanted to go...eventually.

As he neared the house, he noticed Owen out in the corral next to the barn. That was unusual for the middle of the afternoon, especially since Garrett and Wayne weren't around. Wyatt headed that direction.

"You seem as if you're getting around better," Owen said from the back of a chestnut mare.

"Yeah."

"Guess anything's better than ass down on an ambulance stretcher."

"You got that right."

"How much longer you think you'll be staying?"

"Not long. Going to heal enough to where I don't think your sister will throw me back in the hospital if I try to leave."

Owen smiled, and something about that smile made Wyatt antsy.

"Sure it's not more than that?"

"Like what?"

"Maybe you've got a thing for Chloe."

"She's a nice person, been kinder to me than she had any reason to be, but you don't have to worry."

"Did I say anything about being worried? She could do a lot worse."

"And a hell of a lot better." Needing to get off the topic of Chloe, especially with her brother, Wyatt nodded at the horse. "Pretty animal."

Owen patted the side of the mare's neck. "Yeah, hope she'll eventually bring a pretty price, too. I think she's got what it takes to be a barrel racer."

"You train rodeo stock?"

"Going to try. Would do more, but the ranch takes up a lot of time. Now with these damn vandals, the shifts watching for them are eating up even more hours."

"Maybe I can help."

"No offense, man, but I don't think you're in any shape to be chasing after anyone." Owen's mouth edged up at one end. "Unless she wants to be caught."

Wyatt ignored that last part, and instead watched Owen run the horse around a truncated barrel-racing course for a few minutes. Then, leaving the other man to his work, Wyatt wandered into the barn. He inhaled the familiar scents of hay, dirt, leather and horse and instantly felt better than he had in days.

He wasn't willing to give up that feeling anytime soon so he walked down the line of stalls, rubbing the foreheads of the horses that stuck their heads over the stall doors to figure out who this new person was in their territory. He wandered to the opposite side of the barn and stepped into the tack room. There the smell of leather was even stronger, calling to him.

He noticed that in addition to the harnesses and saddles, the room held a surprisingly comfortable-looking bunk and a small fridge and microwave in the corner, likely there for those nights when one of the horses couldn't be left alone. Or maybe at some point a ranch hand had lived in the space.

When he stepped back out into the main aisle of the barn, he felt pretty good, all things considered. He grabbed the pitchfork from where it hung on the wall and started mucking out one of the stalls and tossing in fresh hay. His injuries protested, but he wasn't ready to admit he was doing too much too soon.

"What in the blue Hades are you doing?"

Chapter Eleven

Wyatt spun toward the sound of Chloe's none too happy voice. She stalked into the barn just as he felt a pinch in his middle. He tried to hide it by answering her question.

"Just tossing in a little hay for this guy." He patted the side of the big roan next to him, the one he'd seen Owen astride when he went out to ride the ranch with his brother and dad.

She cursed when she came closer. "And you've re-injured yourself. You're supposed to be getting better, not ripping yourself open again." She closed the rest of the distance between them, jerked the pitchfork out of his hand and hung it back where he'd gotten it. "Come on. Let me fix what you've messed up."

"I wasn't done with the stall." He knew it was a stupid thing to say considering the bloody spot on his shirt right over where Beelzebub had ripped open his side, but she was rubbing him the wrong way.

"Leave it to someone who isn't supposed to be healing from serious injuries and not acting like an idiot."

"Don't treat me like a little kid." His voice snapped like a whip, stopping her in her tracks. He expected her to have a snappy comeback. Instead, she seemed to deflate right in front of him.

"I'm sorry." Her voice sounded shakier than he'd ever heard it. This wasn't like Chloe at all.

He walked toward her, stopping a couple of feet away. "What's wrong?"

She bit her lip and took a breath. "Ruth Carter died today." The moment a tear escaped her eye and flowed down her cheek, he pulled her into his arms, cradling her head against his shoulder. A sob broke free, and he held her even tighter as she cried, stroking her hair in an effort to somehow take away some of her sorrow.

Wyatt, without thinking, dropped a kiss atop her head.

"Chloe, you okay?"

At the sound of Owen's voice, Chloe jumped away from Wyatt as if he'd scorched her skin. "Yeah, fine." She turned her back to her brother and quickly wiped her tears away, pulling all her sorrow inward.

Wyatt doubted she even realized what she was doing, what she'd probably been doing for years right alongside taking care of her family. She was being the strong one, shielding them. It wasn't healthy, and she shouldn't have to shoulder that type of burden alone.

"She lost a patient today," Wyatt said. "Ruth Carter."

The suspicion he'd seen in Owen's eyes faded as he took a few steps into the barn. "Oh, hell. I'm sorry, sis."

Chloe nodded. "She had a good, long life."

And Chloe would miss her, had cared about her. This beautiful woman in front of him had to have the biggest heart of anyone he'd ever met. He wanted to cocoon her in his arms and protect her from anything that might ever try to hurt her again.

"Come on," she said without meeting Wyatt's eyes. "Let's check your stitches." She didn't wait for him to accompany her, instead heading out of the barn without making eye contact with her brother.

When Wyatt started after her, the pain in his side increasing, Owen held out a hand and stopped him. Wyatt expected to get a lecture from Chloe's brother, even though he'd been the one teasing him earlier about having a "thing" for Chloe.

"Thank you," Owen said instead.

"For?"

"Being there for Chloe. She would have never fallen apart like that with one of us, and sometimes she needs to."

Wyatt wouldn't have expected the younger man to be so observant, but he guessed it just showed that often you couldn't tell what a person was really like until they were willing to show you. Still, Wyatt wasn't the one Owen should be telling.

"Maybe you should let her know she doesn't have to shoulder everything alone."

He followed in Chloe's footsteps, not giving Owen time to respond. By the time he heaved himself up the porch steps and trudged into the house, he knew that Chloe had been at least partly right. He wasn't sorry he'd gone for a walk or explored the barn, but he had obviously injured himself again.

Chloe was nowhere to be seen when he stepped into the living room, but he knew she was likely already in the bedroom pulling out her medical supplies. He hated that what he'd done was going to make her work even longer after what had been a bad day.

He stepped into the bedroom and closed the door

behind him. Not wanting this to take any longer than necessary, he removed his shirt and lay down on the bed. Without saying a word, Chloe cleaned the area where he'd popped a stitch and had evidently bumped himself enough to cause a small trickle of blood. After she gave him a local anesthetic, she set to work replacing the stitch. The moment she was done, she stood and started putting her supplies back into the bag.

He carefully got to his feet and crossed the room. He rested his hands on her shoulders and turned her to face him. "I'm sorry."

"I know you didn't do it on purpose, but you've got to trust me when I say you need time to heal, more time than I know you want to give it. You didn't just get a scratch from that bull. You could have died." Her voice broke on the last word, her thoughts probably going back to Ruth.

He pushed her hair back from her tear-streaked face and cupped her jaw, tilting her face upward. "But I didn't, thanks to you. You've cared for me more in the past couple of weeks than… Let's just say I'm not used to it. I'm used to working through the pain because I haven't had a choice." He realized that maybe they weren't all that different.

Before he could tell himself all the reasons it was a bad idea, he lowered his mouth to hers.

A SHOCK WAVE of heat jolted Chloe the moment Wyatt's mouth captured hers. For a split second, she thought that she should pull away, but she shoved that thought aside. She'd had a horrible day, and she'd been fighting her attraction to Wyatt for days, maybe since the first moment he'd been wheeled into her ER. She wanted this, even if it were only temporary.

She moved more fully into his arms and ran her fingers through the hair at the back of his head, pulled him closer. Wyatt made an appreciative sound and deepened the kiss. One of his hands rested between her shoulders while the other slid to the small of her waist. She ran her other hand up his back, feeling the contour of muscles honed from riding bulls.

Chloe inhaled and caught the scent of hay, earth and that intoxicating male scent that made her want to drag him over to her bed and do more than kiss. The tiny sliver of rational thought that remained told her that she couldn't do that, and not just because he was injured.

But it was Wyatt who pulled away, though the hungry look in his eyes and his labored breathing told her he didn't want to. If she had to guess, she'd say he was having thoughts similar to her own.

It wasn't until she'd taken a couple of breaths that she realized why he'd pulled away. The familiar sound of her brothers and dad clunking through the house on the hardwood floors caused her to jump away from Wyatt as if they might have suddenly developed X-ray vision and could see through her bedroom door.

The idea of her dad, Garrett or Owen knowing what she and Wyatt were doing caused her skin to flush hotter than it already was.

"I better go fix dinner."

As she started to walk past Wyatt, he caught her hand, stopping her. She expected him to say something, but he only stared at her for a long moment, his mouth slightly open as if on the verge of speaking, before he simply let her go and broke eye contact.

Instead of being thankful for how easy he was making it to walk away, that empty place inside her grew. Not wanting to examine the reasoning behind that too closely, she hurried from the room.

As she walked into the kitchen, she did her best to act normally. But it had been anything but a normal day. She felt as if she'd just stepped off a day-long roller-coaster ride. Losing Ruth... Chloe couldn't explain why, but it had brought the heartbreaking memories of her mother to the surface. Though she'd lost patients before and would no doubt do so again, she just felt as if every one of her nerve endings were raw. She hated the way someone could be there talking to you one day and the next they were gone forever.

Wyatt walked into the kitchen on the heels of that thought, and she realized she was setting herself up for more heartbreak if she didn't make sure their kiss was a one-time thing, a necessary release after a terrible day.

How had she let him matter to her so much in such a short time? Was it just that he'd wandered into her life as she was beginning to become aware of the empty space inside herself? Or was it more than that? Would he have made the same impression if she'd met him a year ago? When her gaze met and held his for a moment, she knew deep inside that her feelings toward Wyatt had nothing to do with timing.

But it didn't matter, and she had to make sure she wasn't in the position again where they could act on their mutual attraction. It might not bother him when he left to go back to his normal life, but it would her. And yearning for someone she couldn't have wasn't high on her wish list.

She shifted her attention to her dad as he approached. He wrapped an arm around her shoulders and gave her a quick but firm squeeze.

"I'm sorry about Ruth. She was a good woman."

Chloe nodded. "Yes, she was."

As she went about the normal motions of making dinner and setting it on the table, Chloe felt as if her muscles were stretched to the breaking point from the tension of not making eye contact with anyone and trying not to be obvious about that fact. If she met Wyatt's eyes, she feared her flushed skin would give her away. And Owen's gaze? Well, he'd walked in on her in Wyatt's arms in the barn. What was going through his mind about that? Garrett and her father might pick up on the fact that she was nervous and ask why.

She had to force herself to eat so she didn't draw any unwanted questions. But as soon as everyone was done eating and she'd loaded the dishwasher, she knew she couldn't spend the rest of the evening avoiding making eye contact. And she couldn't even retreat to her bedroom since she'd given that to Wyatt. That left one option.

"I'm going to run back to the office for a bit. With everything that happened, I didn't get as much paperwork done as I needed to today."

Her dad looked up from where he was reading the local paper. "You've had a long day. Can't you do it tomorrow?"

"I have a full day tomorrow, too, so it's better if I don't start it already behind."

She'd swear she could feel Wyatt's stare burning into her, but she didn't look in his direction. Instead, she grabbed her purse and headed out the door. As she drove into town, she wondered if she could stay gone until Wyatt and the temptation he presented left Blue Falls behind.

STAYING AT THE home of his doctor was bad enough, but at least Chloe was usually around as a buffer. But with her escape back to town, that left Wyatt in the house with her brothers and dad and feeling more awkward than he had when he'd gotten caught looking at a *Playboy* magazine by his grandma.

Damn, he wished he had his truck. Injuries or not, he'd get out of here before he did something he couldn't take back. The kiss had been great, but also a mistake. And he could tell that Chloe knew that. Buckle bunnies at rodeos didn't mind a kiss from a guy they didn't know just as long as he had on cowboy boots, a hat and snug jeans. But Chloe Brody wasn't that kind of woman. She was the kind who deserved a man who doted on her, who would be there for her every morning when she woke up and every night when she went to sleep, a man who did more than scrimp by and who didn't have convicted felons in his family.

Needing to get outside where he could breathe, he headed out the front door without a word. Considering he'd already reinjured himself once that day, he took it easy as he descended the front steps and walked toward the barn. With each step he took, the pressure in his chest relaxed a bit more.

When he reached the fence that ran alongside the barn all the way to the road, he propped his arms along the top and stared out toward the sunset. He'd never experienced longer days in his life than those since he'd gotten tossed off that bull. While he was happy to not be in the hospital anymore, his days still stretched long and empty. When he'd been working in the barn earlier, that had been the best he'd felt since before his run-in with Beelzebub. But he'd pushed it too far. Three steps forward, two steps back. He wanted to growl like a frustrated animal.

He heard the front door open then close. Looked as if his solitude wasn't going to last long. He was on the verge of taking off for the road, maybe hitching a ride into town, when Chloe's dad stepped up beside him and propped his foot on the bottom slat of the wooden fence.

The older man fixed his gaze on the setting sun, as well. "Doesn't get much prettier than that, does it?"

"No, sir."

Mr. Brody let the silence sit between them. Normally, Wyatt was comfortable not having to make conversation, but something about standing next to Chloe's dad, wondering what was going through the other man's head, made Wyatt want to fidget.

"Heard Chloe had to sew you back up this afternoon."

"Yeah. I didn't mean to cause extra work or concern for her."

"But you were getting stir-crazy sitting around the house doing nothing."

Wyatt glanced at the older man, saw the tan, lined skin of his face and arms that spoke of a lifetime working outdoors. "Yeah."

"I totally understand. I'm a terrible patient myself. So bad that I think my own daughter was on the verge of disowning me."

Wyatt chuckled. "Then it's a wonder she hasn't run me out of the state."

Mr. Brody smiled and tipped the front of his hat up a bit. "Nah. She might fuss a lot, but she does it because she cares, maybe too much."

Wyatt wasn't sure if there were any deeper meaning to Mr. Brody's words. Was he warning Wyatt to not give Chloe reason to care too much for him? No need for that because Wyatt had already sent that message to himself.

Still, he couldn't get the memory of their kiss out of his mind. He'd swear he could still taste her on his lips.

Mr. Brody picked at a loose splinter atop the fence. "She's so much like her mother that sometimes it's hard for me to watch her. That girl has the same big heart, too."

Wyatt searched for something appropriate to say but came up empty. It was all he could do not to fidget.

"You feel like you can drive yet?"

Had Mr. Brody figured out what had happened between him and Chloe earlier? Was he kicking him off the ranch before Chloe could return and protest?

"I believe so, though my truck is still at the fairgrounds."

"No need for that right now. I know you're bored and would much rather be doing something useful, but Chloe will skin us both alive if I have you do something before you're physically ready." Mr. Brody turned toward Wyatt. "I have an order of feed and supplies waiting at the feed store in town. If you think you're up to it, I'll send you to get it tomorrow."

"Sure." The prospect of doing something useful felt great.

Mr. Brody held up his index finger. "But I better not hear of you lifting anything. The guys there can load it for you. You're just the driver."

Wyatt nodded. "Understood. Anything to be of use."

"Good. And even though you won't be doing anything strenuous, I don't think Chloe needs to know, do you?"

Wyatt smiled at the older man's understanding and sneakiness. "No, sir."

Mr. Brody nodded. "Now, since we've got the house to ourselves tonight and we've got a fourth in you, we decided a game of poker sounds good. You any good?"

"What's the right answer here?"

"That you're terrible."

"I stink."

"Just what I wanted to hear." Mr. Brody waved for Wyatt to follow him back to the house.

He tried to focus on the invitation being no more than what it was, an offer of a friendly game. Not an opportunity to feel even more like he could be a part of this family he was growing to like more every day.

Chapter Twelve

"That sounds gorgeous," Chloe said into her phone after listening to her friend Linnea describe every little detail of her wedding dress. She shoved a cold fry from the Primrose in her mouth, a lunch she'd been nibbling on since the fries were still hot.

"Are you okay?"

Chloe stopped writing on the patient file atop her desk at the concern in her friend's voice. "Yes, why?"

"You're responding at all the appropriate places, but you still sound distracted."

Guilt welled up in Chloe. Just because she was working herself half to death so that she didn't have to risk being alone with Wyatt didn't mean she shouldn't be excited for her friend. After all, Linnea had found her Mr. Right and was planning a dream wedding. Chloe was truly happy for Linnea, but talking about her friend's happiness only made her wish more for things she shouldn't. Like Wyatt Kelley, the guy she'd been steering clear of for the past week by working late and leaving her family with a lot of premade dinners.

"Sorry. I'm just up to my eyeballs with work—the usual clinic patients, rounds at the hospital and now this free wellness day we're planning for the community."

"When this wellness day is over, you are taking a weekend off and coming to see me. Or maybe we should go to the beach so you can ogle some hot men. You could use a hot man in your life."

She had one. The problem was he was only passing through.

"I'm so tired right now I wouldn't know what to do with a hot guy if you sat him in front of me."

"Oh, dear, you are in need of a vacation."

Chloe laughed a little at that then made the excuse that she had a patient to see.

"Okay, but be sure you have my wedding on your busy calendar. I'd hate for you to forget you're supposed to be the maid of honor."

"I'm not that bad."

When Chloe finally got off the phone, she picked up another fry but gagged at the idea of eating it. She tossed the rest of the fries into the paper bag her meal had come in and dumped it in the trash can.

Leaving the files to finish later, she walked out of her small office and headed out to where Jenna was just putting a patient file in the bin next to one of the examination rooms.

"A heads-up, it's Verona in there. And she's got that dangerous sparkle in her eyes."

Chloe sighed. "Just what I need."

"She's already mentioned Wyatt, said that Adam Johnson saw him at the feed store the other day getting a load in your dad's truck."

Chloe froze. "What?"

"You didn't know?"

She shook her head. Of course, she'd barely seen Wyatt in passing the past few days. What did she expect if she wasn't there to tell him to take it easy? Honestly, she was surprised that if he could drive he hadn't left yet. A little part of her wanted to believe the reason had nothing to do with his healing process and everything to do with that kiss they'd shared. The kiss she hadn't given him a chance to repeat.

"Thanks for the warning." She put on her game face and headed into the exam room. "Hey, Verona. What seems to be the problem today?"

"I've got some ringing in my ear."

"Well, let's take a look." She grabbed the otoscope and looked into Verona's left ear, already suspecting she wouldn't find anything.

"How's the planning for the wellness fair going?"

"Good. We just have a few more things to wrap up and wrangle a couple more volunteers."

"Maybe Wyatt could help. He must be doing better."

Chloe felt like smacking herself upside the head. She'd stepped right into that one. "Like most things, his type of injuries get a little better every day."

"Doesn't hurt to have your own personal doctor making sure everything is going well. You must have the healing touch if he's already up on a horse."

"On a horse?" Chloe's voice was a little loud and a lot more surprised than it should have been, but she didn't care. She was damned close to racing home and telling Wyatt Kelley just how big of an idiot he was if what Verona said was true.

"Yeah. David Finch was doing the electric meter readings out your way this morning and said he saw Wyatt out with Owen in the corral."

Chloe reined in her emotions and sat the otoscope on the countertop. "I don't see anything wrong with your ear. Have you been on the phone a lot today?"

"A bit."

Chloe wanted to laugh. Verona's cell phone carrier was losing its collective shirt by giving the woman unlimited minutes. "Maybe go easy on the phone for the next day or so, and the ringing should go away."

Verona's mouth quirked in a way that told Chloe the older woman knew she'd been caught in her fib. Chloe couldn't help but smile at Verona's determination.

By the time the end of the day rolled around, Chloe couldn't decide if she were more tired or irked that Wyatt evidently hadn't learned his lesson when he'd popped the stitch while working in the barn. But as she drove home, she told herself she'd done all she could. If he were determined to reinjure himself, then that was his decision. But he could do it somewhere other than under her roof.

When she got home, she saw Wyatt standing under the open hood of Garrett's truck. Great, now he was doing auto repair. Men were idiots.

She made up her mind to just ignore Wyatt, let him do whatever he wanted, but the moment she stepped out of the car she couldn't help herself. She marched up to him and crossed her arms.

"So, how many stitches have you popped today?"

He looked at her with confusion knitting his brow. "Did I do something to tick you off?"

"After I told you that you needed time to recover, even after I had to stitch you up again, I hear you're loading feed and riding horses."

Wyatt slowly turned toward her and leaned one hand

against the front of the truck. "You need to get your facts right before you start making accusations."

"So you weren't at the feed store the other day?"

"I was. Your dad asked me to pick up a load. I figured it was the least I could do to repay his hospitality. Not that you care, but I didn't load one ounce of the supplies. I just drove the truck there and back."

Chloe hated the feeling of being wrong, but part of her still told her that she wasn't. "And the horse riding?"

"Yes, I got on a horse this morning. Sitting around your house doing nothing isn't going to help me get back to riding form. Every day I sit around on my ass, it's one day closer to the end of the year and one more day I don't make one red cent. If I want to get back to riding anytime soon, I've got to push myself some."

Chloe threw up her hands. "You're not going to be riding anymore this year, you daft man. If you had a lick of sense, you wouldn't climb on a bull ever again."

"Damn it, Chloe. It's all I know!"

Something about the way he said those words, as if some part of him were ashamed, tore at her heart, a heart she realized had been making more and more room for him every day, even when she barely saw him.

"You're not so old that you can't learn something else."

"Why are you being so unreasonable about this? Why do you even care?"

"Because you damn near died, and you might not be so lucky next time." She felt tears forming at the idea of him being gored to death and hurried toward the house before she let them fall in front of him.

She made it to the bathroom before she lost the battle and the tears overflowed. She swiped at them, angry that she'd allowed herself to care so much for someone who was going to leave. He'd made that painfully obvious with his insistence that he needed to get better so he could return to riding those damned bulls.

Also obvious was that she no longer thought of him as only a patient. Somewhere during their Scrabble games and his failed cooking attempts and their butting heads over his recovery, she'd begun to fall for him. She slid to the floor and realized she was every bit the fool he was, only for a different reason. He was a fool because he wanted to leave, and she was because she wanted him to stay.

THAT BEACH WEEKEND with Linnea was sounding better every day. Not wanting to endure the embarrassment of facing Wyatt after her meltdown, Chloe stayed at work even longer the next day, so long in fact that her family was already in bed when she came home. She had no idea if Wyatt was still awake, but it didn't matter. By the time she climbed the porch steps, she was too exhausted to walk the rest of the way into the house. Instead, she sank into one of the rocking chairs and closed her eyes.

Roscoe nuzzled her hand, and she wrestled up enough energy to give him a couple of scratches between his floppy ears. She'd just sit here for a few minutes, gather up enough willpower to force herself the final few feet to the couch.

She knew she'd made a mistake when she felt herself drifting toward sleep. And yet she wasn't able to do anything to correct it. Maybe if she took a little nap…

When she woke, something was different. It took a

couple of blinks for her to realize that night had given way to the dawning of another day. She'd slept all night on the porch in a rocking chair. The moment she lifted her head away from the back of the chair, her body protested its rough treatment.

Movement out of the corner of her eye turned out to be her dad sitting in the other rocking chair drinking his morning coffee.

"It's time you stopped avoiding Wyatt," he said in his no-nonsense way.

She started to deny it, but then he looked at her with an expression that she knew all too well. It was the same one he'd worn whenever he'd caught one of his kids in a lie, a combination of warning and disappointment.

"I know you've fallen for him. I recognize the signs. You look at him the same way I looked at your mother, as if you can't imagine living another day without him."

"It doesn't matter. He doesn't feel the same way."

"Are you sure about that?"

"He has no plans of staying. Almost every one of our disagreements has been because he can't wait to get out of here and back on the rodeo circuit." Back to where he stood a good chance of riding one too many bulls and either getting killed or injured beyond repair.

"He can drive now. Why hasn't he left?"

"His truck is in town."

"Easily remedied if he truly wanted to leave."

She sighed. "I don't know. Maybe something I said finally sank in."

"He's a good man, Chloe. A lot of people are takers, but he's not. He's determined to help around here to pay his way."

"And he thinks it'll get him back atop a bull sooner."

Her dad took another drink of his coffee and was quiet for several moments. "Maybe the boy just needs a reason to stick around other than a doctor's orders." He shifted his gaze back to her. "You're always so busy taking care of everyone around you. It's about time you did something for yourself."

"I did, when I went to college and med school."

Her dad was already shaking his head before she finished speaking. "That may be partially true, but I also know you did it to help out me and your brothers." He let out a long sigh and looked out to where the sun was rising in the east. "You shouldered too much responsibility too early, and that's my fault. I took the easy way out and let you step into your mother's shoes. I never let you just be a normal kid, a normal teenager."

"Dad—"

He held up his hand, stopping her. "You've been selfless for too long, honey. It's time you do something selfish, go after what you want."

As if on cue, Wyatt walked out of the barn. What was he doing out there already? Had he walked right past her sleeping on the porch?

Her dad caught the direction of her gaze. "Wyatt moved out to the room in the barn yesterday."

"Why'd he do that when there's a perfectly good bed inside the house?"

"Because he knew you were staying away because of him, because he was in your space."

"He said that?"

"He didn't have to."

She glanced back at Wyatt just as he looked toward her. Their gazes held for a moment before she lowered hers. The kiss they'd shared indicated that Wyatt at least found her attractive, but she doubted there was anything she could do to make him stay. He'd said multiple times that rodeo was his life. And despite her fears for his safety, she didn't have the right to ask him to give it up. It'd be the same as if he asked her to stop practicing medicine.

"I'm not butting in only for you." Her dad nodded toward where Wyatt was heading back into the barn. "There's an aloneness about that boy that feels almost like self-punishment. From what I've seen of him, he doesn't deserve that." He shifted his attention back to Chloe. "Neither one of you deserves to be alone."

Chloe was stunned into silence at both her dad's perceptiveness and the fact that he was offering relationship advice. As he stood and headed into the house, she wondered if he were thinking about her mom and how alone he'd been since her death.

Long after her dad rode off with her brothers toward the far end of the ranch, she still didn't know what the right move was with Wyatt. Part of her wanted to march into the barn and finish what they'd started in her bedroom, but would that just make it hurt worse when Wyatt left? Or if she didn't satisfy her yearning for him, would she regret it for the rest of her life?

Those questions were still bouncing around in her head, unanswered, when she dragged herself to yet another day of work.

She was so distracted all day that she called people by the wrong names, forgot to return phone calls, even nearly put her keys in the lock of the wrong car when she finally left for the night. Despite all that, she had almost everything ready for the wellness fair. If only figuring out the right move with Wyatt were so easy.

She started home just as the sun was sinking below the horizon. Her thoughts drifted back to her conversation with her dad that morning and how she'd wondered throughout the day how her dad had survived all these years without the woman who'd owned his whole heart. Had he endured loneliness so strong that he was able to see the same in others? Is that why he'd been able to peg Wyatt's? And hers?

Instead of driving straight home, she turned onto Hillcrest Drive. When she walked into the cemetery a couple minutes later, she wasn't surprised to see a fresh bouquet of pink roses in the vase on her mother's headstone. She sank onto her knees next to the grave and ran her fingertips over the soft petals of the roses. Even after all these years, she remembered the smell of the rose-scented lotion her mother used.

"Hi, Mom." She stared at the words on her mother's stone, the name, the dates of birth and death, *Beloved wife and mother.* How she wished her mom were with her now to tell her the right path to take, to know whether opening up her heart to Wyatt was a risk worth taking.

A soft breeze stirred the ribbons on a wreath atop the next grave then wafted past Chloe's cheeks. She imagined it was her mother's hands caressing her.

"I don't know what to do," she said. "I…care about Wyatt, even though that might sound crazy." But it was true. From the moment she'd met him, she'd felt drawn to him as if by some otherworldly force.

Of all the men in the world, why him? Why could she not push thoughts of him out of her mind? Why was it so hard to admit that her efforts to keep him safe, her insistence that he take it easy and recover, wasn't only because of their doctor-patient relationship. Perhaps too much had to do with the fact that she simply didn't want him to leave.

It was as if the two halves of herself were locked in a battle of wills—one half yearning to give in to her attraction, the other afraid that if she did she'd end up as hurt and alone as her father.

She looked at the words *Beloved wife* etched into the stone and realized that it would have been a lot sadder if her parents had not ever allowed themselves to be together for fear of eventually being hurt. They'd had a good marriage, had loved each other very much, had made a lot of wonderful memories together. She doubted her dad regretted one moment of those years when he'd still had the woman he loved, that he wouldn't give it up in exchange for the assurance he'd never have to grieve.

Chloe's breath caught in her throat. The absolute certainty that she'd regret it if Wyatt left without her being honest with him hit her so hard it almost knocked her over. She placed her hand atop the stone and smiled. "Thanks, Mom."

She ran back to her car, suddenly very scared that she'd waited too long, that she'd missed her opportunity.

Chapter Thirteen

Wyatt shoved the last of his clean laundry into his bag and jerked the zipper shut. No matter what he'd done all day, he couldn't rid himself of the frustration and anger that were fighting for dominance within him. Frustration that he hadn't been able to hold Chloe in his arms again and anger that he even wanted to.

He knew her pulling away was for the best, and he ought to be thanking her. After all, there could be nothing between them long-term. She was a good, loving person from a good, hardworking family. He could only imagine how she'd react if she knew that he was the only offspring of convicted felons.

So in the morning, he would ask her dad or one of her brothers for a ride into town. He'd get in his truck and drive away until Blue Falls was nothing but a memory and the place where he owed a rather large medical bill. He'd leave Chloe free to find a man who was good enough for her, who could make her as happy as she deserved to be, one who didn't frustrate her like he did.

Unable to stand still, he left his temporary living quarters and walked out of the back of the barn and through the gate that led out into the cattle pasture. It was getting dark, but it felt way better to be out under the emerging stars than in that cramped room.

He ambled up the hill that rose as the ranch stretched off to the west. He wondered what it would be like to be as attached to a piece of land as the Brodys obviously were to their home. Though he called Laramie home, he could barely remember a time when he'd lived in one place more than two or three months at a stretch. He found himself wishing he could know, just once, how it felt to have a place be so important that it was like a part of him.

He stopped and looked out across the land, though he couldn't make out much in the dark now. Except… there was movement down by the fence. He strained to see more clearly. Instead he heard hushed voices. He glanced over his shoulder and realized he'd walked farther than he'd thought. The lights of the house were no longer visible.

Careful not to make noise, he eased down the hill toward where he saw dark shapes moving against a darker background. He knew in his gut what he was going to find even before he saw more movement in the field then heard the sound of cattle hooves shuffling against the ground.

"What was that?"

This time, Wyatt heard the words clearly and realized he'd been seen. In the next moment, he heard a slap then the cattle started moving toward the fence. Only Wyatt suspected the fence was cut. The figure in the field started running.

Oh, hell no. These bastards weren't getting away with this, not again. Regardless of the pain it caused him, Wyatt hurried toward the cut in the fence. He cursed as he tripped. He managed to right himself before he fell, but the pain ripping through him stole his breath. He was forced to take a few moments to let the pain recede enough that he could move again.

He heard two car doors shut, one after the other, and then a motor start. Damn, they were going to get away.

Wyatt saw cattle stepping through the fence and got an idea. Pushing past the pain, he went against common sense and slapped several cows on their rears, urging them into the road, cutting off one means of escape. He hurried after them, skidding to a stop in the middle of the road. Right at that moment, headlights approaching from the opposite direction bathed everything in light. Unfortunately, the driver of the getaway truck laid down on his horn and lurched forward, causing the cattle to scatter out of his way.

"No!" Wyatt ran after the truck until he doubled over with the pain.

The car behind him thankfully stopped before he got pancaked.

"Wyatt?"

He held his stomach as he turned toward the sound of Chloe's panicked voice. She ran toward him, and when he saw the fear on her face something slipped into place inside him like a long-lost puzzle piece that finally found its way into the right spot. She nearly collided with him, only pulling herself up short at the last moment.

"Are you okay? Are you hurt?" She grabbed his upper arm and scanned him from head to toe.

"I'm fine. Hurt like hell, but I'm not going to spill my guts in the middle of the road." He glanced toward the cattle milling about. "We've got to get these cows out of the road before someone else comes along and hits one."

She didn't argue, but instead hurried alongside him while she called the house for backup. They flanked the cattle and herded them back toward the cut fence. Every time he thought they were about to drive them all in the right direction, one or two would slip off the wrong way. His middle was hurting so much he thought he might throw up. He'd been healing well lately, but running and herding cows on foot weren't exactly on the approved list of activities yet.

He heard the sound of approaching hooves down the road and turned to see Chloe's brothers approaching on horseback, followed by their dad in his truck. With their help, it only took a few more minutes to get the cattle back on the correct side of the fence. As soon as they were safely corralled, Mr. Brody pulled a roll of barbed wire and a toolbox out of the bed of his truck, and he, Owen and Garrett got to work stringing new fencing.

Spent, Wyatt grabbed hold of the side of the truck to keep from giving in to the urge to bend double. Instead, he gritted his teeth and managed to bring his breathing under control.

"I need to get you back to the house," Chloe said as she came to stand in front of him.

"In a minute."

"What were you doing out here anyway?"

"Went for a walk. Happened upon this, and it was too far to go back for help."

"Wish I'd seen them instead," Garrett said, anger evident in his voice. "I would have been hard-pressed not to run them over."

"They're getting bolder," Mr. Brody said. "They've never cut a fence this close to a house before. Did you happen to see what they were driving?"

For the first time all day, Wyatt smiled. "Better. I got the license plate number."

Everyone stood still for a moment before Owen hooted and they all started laughing.

When Chloe pulled up in front of the house a few minutes later, Wyatt felt as if someone had whacked him across the stomach with a two-by-four. By the time he managed to scoot himself out of her car, she was already there for him to lean on.

"I'm fine," he said.

"And my name's Thelma Lou."

"Nice to meet you, Thelma."

"Oh, hush." She grabbed his arm and wrapped it around her shoulder then headed for the front porch steps.

He stopped. "I think you're going the wrong way."

"Nope. You're sleeping in the house tonight instead of that awful bunk in the barn."

"It's not awful. I've slept in worse."

"I don't care if you've slept on a bed of nails before. There's no sense in you sleeping out there when there's a perfectly good bed in the house."

"A bed that belongs to you."

Chloe opened her mouth to argue again, but he pressed his finger to her lips. With a sigh, she gave up but didn't release him. Rather, she simply changed directions and escorted him to the barn.

The moment they stepped into his small room, she froze. "You're leaving?"

"It's time."

"But your injuries, they're not healed all the way. And you probably did more damage tonight."

Wyatt broke contact with Chloe and walked to the opposite side of the small room. "I've imposed on your family's hospitality long enough."

"It's not imposing if I invited you."

"Chloe, it's obvious that I wore out my welcome days ago."

"That's not true."

"So you ignore all your guests?"

"I…" She seemed at a loss for words, and he could almost see the frantic search for them going on in her pretty head. And then she lifted her gaze to his. "I don't want you to go." She swallowed. "Not yet."

Damn if his heart didn't skip a beat. Standing there staring at her, he wanted to forget all the reasons why he couldn't have her.

She took a tentative step toward him, then another, and he couldn't find the willpower to stop her. "Please let me check to make sure you didn't reinjure yourself."

Of course, she never stopped being the concerned doctor. What had he thought she meant to do when she reached him?

He obliged by lifting the edge of his shirt. He stared over the top of her head as she examined his wounds, but his breath caught when her hand lingered on his stomach. Wyatt lowered his gaze just as she lifted hers. The last of his willpower fled like a leaf on a gusty breeze, and he lifted his hand to frame her face.

"Are my injuries the only reason you don't want me to leave?"

Chloe swallowed then licked her lips. He imagined he could see a battle going on in her eyes.

"No."

He pulled her close and lowered his mouth to hers. Immediately, his blood started pumping faster. He'd steered away from drugs all his life, afraid he'd follow in his parents' footsteps, but Chloe was proving to be more intoxicating than any drug ever could be.

"Wait," she said as she pulled back. "I don't want to hurt you."

"Chloe, stop worrying and let me kiss you."

He did exactly that, losing himself in the feminine scent of her, the feel of her curves beneath his hands, the taste of her warm mouth. He backed her up until she was pressed against the wall. When her hands slid up over his chest, he growled into her mouth.

That seemed to light a fire in her because in the next instant she was unbuttoning his shirt.

"What are you doing?"

She smiled against his lips. "I'd think that was obvious."

"You're making it damned hard to resist you."

"Then stop trying."

They were both careful of his injuries, but they still managed to send clothing flying in all directions. Wyatt grabbed his packed bag and tossed it in the far corner. He eased down onto the bed then tugged Chloe's hand so she'd join him.

When they were stretched out along the narrow bunk, he caressed her soft check. "You're so beautiful. I can't imagine why you're here with me."

"Don't tell me you haven't been with beautiful women before."

"None like you."

"I've seen the girls who hang out at rodeos, hoping to score a cowboy. I'm nothing special."

"That's where you're wrong."

He ran his hand up her side, coming to rest next to her breast. He skimmed the soft fabric of her bra with his thumb then lowered his mouth to the mound that rose above it. Chloe sucked in a breath and arched toward him, making him go even harder.

Wyatt kissed her all the way up her neck then nuzzled her ear. "I know I should pull away, but I want you."

After all, every man had his limits, and he'd reached his for resisting Chloe Brody.

CHLOE NEARLY CRIED out when Wyatt rolled away from her. No, she couldn't be this close, have finally given herself permission to be with him, even if it were for only one night, to have him turn away. But she kept the words and feelings inside, and wondered how she could get dressed and leave the room without melting from the heat of her embarrassment.

Before she could formulate a plan, he was back beside her, stretching his long body next to hers. Then she realized what he'd done, protecting them both.

"What's wrong?" he asked as he caressed her cheek.

"I thought you were having second thoughts."

"I should, but I'm not."

She smiled. "Good."

For one night, she was going to stop thinking rationally and enjoy herself. She just hoped her dad and brothers stayed far away from the barn.

Wyatt shifted, edging his leg between hers. He pulled her close and captured her mouth with his.

Somewhere in the midst of the kiss, he freed her of her bra and panties. The sensation of skin on skin only increased her need to be as close to Wyatt at possible.

When Wyatt moved atop her, he paused and gently swept her hair away from her face. The way he looked at her—as if she were the most beautiful, precious thing in the world—made her heart swell. And in that moment she knew she was falling in love with him. She couldn't allow herself to think about how much it was going to hurt when he left. If she let those thoughts into her head, she wouldn't be able to enjoy what would likely be her only chance of being truly held in his arms, of being able to love him in this one small way.

When he captured her mouth again, she wasn't able to wait any longer. She lifted her body toward his, and he slid into hers. She moaned into his mouth, and his hands found and entwined with hers as he started to move. Wyatt broke the kiss but used those talented lips to scorch a path down her neck until he found her breast. A flick of his tongue across the tip caused her to gasp and press him more firmly to her.

That action seemed to spur him to move faster. As he filled her with a pleasure she'd never truly known, she threw her head back. Her release built with each stroke, and she dug her fingers into the muscles of Wyatt's back. Her breaths came shorter and closer together as she got closer and closer. When the release finally came, she couldn't help the loud moan of pleasure. Wyatt made a couple more strokes before his entire body stiffened with his own release.

When he collapsed beside her, she smiled so wide she wouldn't be surprised if she pulled a facial muscle. But then a sliver of common sense wormed its way into her brain, concern that he might have pushed himself way too hard tonight.

"Tell me the truth," she said as she placed her hand against the slight stubble on his cheek. "Are you okay?"

Wyatt placed his warm hand at the curve of her hip and gave her a satisfied smile. "Haven't felt this good in ages. I think you have the healing touch, Doc."

She tried to playfully swat him, but he caught her hand and brought it to his lips, kissing each finger in turn while holding her gaze.

They kissed for a long time as Wyatt held her close. She knew she should dress and go in the house, but she just couldn't force herself out of his arms. She was afraid that if she left his side, in the morning when she woke he'd be gone.

Not wanting to think about that yet, she snuggled close to him, willing to stay as long as he'd let her. With her head next to his chest, she listened to his steady heartbeat and thought that she wouldn't mind listening to it every day for the rest of her life.

CHLOE WOKE TO the sound of laughter. Her first instinct was panic, until she remembered that she'd eased her way back into the house and her own bedroom in the middle of the night. She glanced at the clock, stunned to see it was an hour past when she normally woke each morning. Good thing it was one of her days off.

Despite the time, she lay in bed reliving every moment of the night before, from when her headlights had illuminated Wyatt in the middle of the road to when she'd felt herself drifting asleep in his arms. When she'd awakened a few hours later, he'd tried to get her to stay. But the idea of being caught by her dad or brothers mortified her. The long, thorough kiss he'd given her at the door to his little room nearly changed her mind.

As she'd crossed the distance between the barn and the house, she'd imagined it being the miles that lay between Texas and Wyoming.

Was Wyatt gone already? She bit her lip at that thought, but the loss wasn't going to get any easier just because she was lying in her room avoiding it.

So she forced herself out of bed and headed for the bathroom. As the water ran over her skin, she imagined it was Wyatt's hands again. He'd been wrong when he'd said that riding bulls was the only thing he knew how to do. Though she'd only been with a handful of men, Wyatt was far and away the best lover she'd ever had. And that was with him injured. Her body heated at the idea of what he might be like if he didn't have to be careful of his injuries. Not that he'd been overly cautious the night before. He hadn't left her wanting.

Before she went up in flames, Chloe got out of the shower and finished getting ready. When she opened the bathroom door, Wyatt stood on the other side, a smile tugging at his lips.

"Good morning, finally."

"You're still here." She heard the relief in her voice and didn't care if he did, too. After last night, there couldn't be any doubt that she enjoyed being with him.

"I am."

She glanced past him down the hallway.

"They're already gone."

"Oh."

Wyatt wrapped his arm around her waist and pulled her close. "Are you nervous to be alone with me, Doc? Afraid I might have my way with you?"

Feeling mischievous, she looked up into his beautiful eyes. "Tease."

The kiss he laid on her nearly caused her legs to buckle.

"It's not a tease if I deliver."

They stood in the hall kissing until Chloe knew she either had to head to the kitchen, or they were going to end up in her bed. She'd managed to not get caught the night before, but she wasn't risking it again. At least not in her family's home.

She reluctantly broke the kiss and edged past Wyatt. "I've got to have some coffee."

Wyatt followed her. "Tiring night?"

She glanced over her shoulder at him. "Nah, not much going on."

Wyatt narrowed his eyes at her before picking up his pace. She squealed like a little kid and raced for the kitchen. He caught up to her and backed her against the countertop for another long, wonderful kiss.

"So what are we going to do today?" His words felt warm and suggestive against her wet lips.

"You're not leaving?"

"Not today. The road will still be there tomorrow."

She tried not to let it show just how happy that news made her, at least the part about him staying one more day. "You feel up to a ride around the ranch?"

"You're actually suggesting I do something besides sit on the front porch?"

"Yep, you're still ornery." She turned to retrieve two travel mugs from the cabinet and filled them with coffee.

Wyatt stepped up behind her and wrapped his arms around her shoulders. "I'd love to go for a ride."

Several minutes later, she had two horses saddled and ready to go. She watched as Wyatt clenched his jaw when he pulled himself onto the horse, but she didn't ask if he was okay. He was actually healing well considering the state he'd been in when he arrived at the hospital. Maybe all that bullheaded determination did work after all.

Chloe led the way, taking a familiar trail that led to one of the higher spots on the ranch where you could see for miles. They didn't talk as they rode, but Chloe found the silence between them oddly comfortable. She caught herself smiling, happy to be spending the day out under the wide open sky with a man who had unknowingly filled that yawning empty spot within her. She flatly refused to think about how much bigger that emptiness was going to be when Wyatt left.

Give him a reason to stay.

Her dad's words echoed in her mind again, but she couldn't ask that of Wyatt. She didn't have the right.

When they reached the vantage point she wanted him to see, she pulled her mount to a halt.

"I think your dad should have built his house here," Wyatt said as he stopped beside her.

"It's my favorite spot on the ranch. It's not as high as some areas in the Hill Country, but I've always felt like I was on top of the world. I used to come up here after Mom died. Everyone told me she was in heaven, so I felt like I was closer to her here. I'd sit for hours."

"That's how I was whenever Grandpa would take me fishing. He had this favorite bend in the Snake River, and I still think it's the prettiest place I've ever seen."

"Did your dad go, too?"

"No." His answer was fast, clipped, like all his answers to questions about his parents. But he must have realized how sharp he'd been because he glanced at her then sighed. "My dad wasn't around. I was raised by my grandparents."

She wanted to know more, but she didn't want to ruin what could be their last day together by pressing for information he might not want to share.

They sat in silence for a few seconds, watching the grazing cattle and a hawk soaring high above.

Wyatt shifted on his horse. "You're lucky to have this. And a family that's so close."

Though she didn't know the details about his family, she saw that aloneness her dad had mentioned and it broke her heart.

"I am. I try not to forget that."

After a couple more minutes gazing out at the expanse of the ranch, Chloe pointed her horse toward the trail that meandered back toward the house. But when she reached the small stream that eventually emptied out into Blue Falls Lake, she reined in and dismounted.

She looked up at Wyatt as he approached. "Hungry?"

"I don't think you're going to catch any fish in that stream."

She smiled. "Good thing for you I brought some sandwiches, then."

"Scenery and sandwiches. I'm either being bribed or seduced."

Heat flooded Chloe's cheeks. She turned away and hoped she could blame it on the bright April sun. Was she trying to coerce him into staying without realizing it?

Without looking at him, she sat next to the creek

and pulled out the sandwiches. When he joined her, she extended a wrapped sandwich to him. "Hope you like ham and cheese."

"Sounds great."

He seemed to be a man who was easy to please. If only he could be happy with a simple life in a small town. But how did someone who'd spent most of his life on the road settle down? Would they even know how?

She thought of Logan Bradshaw, Skyler's husband. He'd been a confirmed rodeo rider until he'd fallen head over heels for Skyler and their baby.

Chloe shifted her gaze downstream. Wyatt wasn't Logan, and she wasn't Skyler. And there was no baby to help cement the relationship. Though she did believe that Logan would have given up his life on the circuit for Skyler alone. Chloe actually ached when she saw how Logan looked at Skyler, the same way so many of her friends' husbands looked at them. Maybe Verona had put something in the Blue Falls water supply because it sure seemed there'd been a lot of happy matches in the past couple of years.

Instead of diving into his sandwich, he set it aside and lowered his mouth to hers. While their kisses earlier had been heated and hungry, this time they were soft and tender, paving the way for him to waltz right into the center of her heart.

Some sense of self-preservation allowed her to pull away.

Wyatt ran his thumb over her lower lip. "What's wrong?"

"I... Last night was great, but I don't want to let this go too far since you're leaving, which is okay. I understand your life is elsewhere."

He stared at her for several moments, as if memorizing the contours of her face. "I don't know what the future holds. I never do. But sometimes it's just nice to live in the moment and not worry about what's going to happen tomorrow."

She opened her mouth to say...something, but then she realized she'd had much the same thought the night before when she'd made the decision to make love to him.

He must have seen her about to relent because in the next instant he was laying her back in the grass and kissing her. Her blood began to hum, and she wondered what it'd be like to make love out here under the bright blue sky.

They were getting so into each other that it took her a moment to realize why he suddenly pulled away. She'd never hated a cell phone so much in her life.

Chapter Fourteen

Wyatt nearly tossed the phone in the creek, but then he saw who was calling and answered.

"Hello?"

"Is this Wyatt Kelley?"

"Yes."

"This is Erma Cavanaugh at Mountain View Nursing Center. I'm sorry to have to tell you this, but your grandfather passed away a short time ago."

If he'd been hit in the chest with a cannonball, it couldn't have hurt any more. And that didn't make sense, not really, because in all honesty his grandfather had been gone a long time. At least the man he'd once been.

"Mr. Kelley?"

"Yes, I'm here. I mean, I'm in Texas right now, but I'll be there as soon as I can."

He somehow mumbled his way through the answers to some questions, the ones Erma probably had asked countless other family members over the years. For a crazy, detached moment, he wondered if she had nightmares about those questions.

When he finally hung up, he startled when Chloe

wrapped her hand around his. He'd somehow forgotten she was there.

"Your grandpa?"

He nodded. "He died this morning." He didn't know
why he'd said it. The topic of his conversation with
Erma couldn't have been mistaken even just hearing
the one side. "I have to go."

He got to his feet and headed toward his horse before he remembered he should do the gentlemanly thing
and help her to her feet. But by the time he'd turned
around, she was already slipping her foot into her stir-
rup and pulling herself astride.

The ride back to the ranch was less leisurely than the
ride out but just as quiet. He was lost in memories of
his grandfather and all the details he had to deal with
in the days ahead. Chloe probably just didn't know the
right thing to say, and he couldn't fault her for that.
What could a person say other than they were sorry?
And the look on her face and the way she'd held his
hand had already said that.

When they reached the barn, he realized his middle was aching from the ride. He hated to think what
kind of pain he'd be in by the time he drove all the
way to Laramie.

"Give me a few minutes to pack a bag."

He looked at Chloe, confused. "What?"

She met his eyes and he saw a determination there
that he'd seen outside the hospital that day he'd tried
to leave on his own.

"I'm going with you."

"To Wyoming?"

"Yes, to Wyoming."

"Chloe, that doesn't make any sense. You didn't even know my grandpa."

"No, but I know you. And no one should be alone to deal with something like this."

He started to protest again, needing to keep her out of that part of his life. He'd probably made a mistake letting her in as much as he had, though he had to admit she'd made his heart feel lighter than he'd ever thought possible.

Chloe held up her hand. "You know better than to argue with me. I can be every bit as stubborn as you. And if you take off without me, I'm just going to follow you all the way there."

He didn't doubt her one bit.

Hours later, he woke up to find it was dark outside his truck. He turned his head to see Chloe with one hand on the wheel and the other arm propped along the edge of the door. She looked tired.

He still couldn't believe that she was with him, that she'd put her life on hold in order to travel a thousand miles with someone who hadn't promised her anything beyond one night together and some really hot kisses. He wanted so much to be worthy of her because in that moment he knew he loved her. He was crazy, stupid in love with Chloe Brody.

As if she sensed he'd awakened, she glanced at him. "Hey, you woke up just in time to pump gas."

He looked out the windshield to see she was getting off at an exit with a truck stop lighting up the night. "Where are we?"

"Outskirts of Pueblo, Colorado."

He straightened in his seat. "Sorry I slept so long."

"You needed it."

He looked back at her. "You need to rest now."

"I'm okay."

"Either you let me drive my own truck when we leave here or I'm not getting in."

She looked at him and laughed. "I guess it is your turn to be stubborn."

After they went to the bathroom, filled up the truck with gas and loaded up on caffeine and food, they hit the road again. Despite the soda she'd drank, it wasn't long before Chloe curled up in the corner of the passenger side and fell asleep.

Wyatt glanced over at her and smiled before returning his attention to the road. Soon they would go their separate ways, but tonight she was still with him. He could still smell her delicate feminine scent and hear her soft breathing. And it felt right. It wouldn't last, but for now he was going to pretend it could. Tomorrow, he'd have to face the reality of his grandfather's death. That was soon enough to cut the final tie with Chloe. Might as well get all the hurt over with at once.

CHLOE HADN'T REALIZED how hard the trip to Wyoming was going to be. She'd been to several funerals since her mother's, but making the arrangements for one? That was a whole different story. But she hid how her insides shrank away from every decision Wyatt had to make because he shouldn't have to do it alone.

Still, by the time their meeting with the funeral director was over, she had to excuse herself. She hurried to the restroom and splashed water on her face. The combination of fatigue, hunger and emotions tugged to the surface had her feeling shaky.

She lost track of how long she stood over the sink,

staring at herself in the mirror. But if she were drained, Wyatt had to be even more so, considering he was doing everything while recovering from serious injuries.

When she stepped out into the hallway, Wyatt was waiting for her.

"You okay?"

"Yeah, just tired."

"You can go home now," he said. "I'll drive you to the airport, and—"

She stepped forward and took his hands in hers. "Wyatt, stop. I'm not going anywhere."

He looked at her as if he couldn't believe what he was seeing. "You're amazing."

"I'm just doing what any decent person would."

"No. Decent people send their condolences, flowers. They don't drive through the night just to be there for someone they barely know."

She ran her thumb across the back of one of his hands. "Maybe it doesn't feel like I barely know you anymore."

He stared at Chloe for a long moment before he gathered her close and just held her.

Several minutes later, they walked hand in hand to his truck. It felt so natural, as if they'd known and cared for each other much longer than they actually had. Once they were in the truck and leaving the parking lot, Wyatt reached across the seat and took her hand again. It was as if he needed the physical contact, and she wasn't about to deny him. The truth was she found every bit as much comfort in their connection as he likely did.

She expected they were headed to a motel, so she

was surprised when he pulled into the short driveway beside a small house that looked several decades old. The way he'd talked, she didn't think he had a home anywhere. But he didn't have to tell her this was his grandfather's house, that this was where he'd been raised.

He sat so long staring out the windshield that she wondered if he would ever get out of the truck. But she didn't rush him, didn't even speak.

"I haven't been here in a long time," he finally said. "Only once or twice since Grandpa went into the home. Because of the Alzheimer's, he probably didn't even remember he had a house. But I just couldn't get rid of it. I guess some dumb part of me kept hoping he'd get better and come back."

Chloe squeezed his hand. "It's not dumb. It just shows how much you loved him."

Wyatt took a shaky breath. "He didn't even know me anymore."

"But you knew him. That's what matters."

Wyatt looked across the truck toward her. "I'm glad you're here."

She showed him a small smile. "Me, too."

They were both so tired that they fell asleep within moments of curling onto a bed that she suspected had been Wyatt's when he was a boy. When she woke, she walked down to the corner where there was a fast-food restaurant and got them something to eat. When she returned, Wyatt was standing in the middle of the living room scanning his surroundings.

"You okay?"

He shifted his attention to her. "Yeah. Just thinking how quickly I can go through all this and get the house on the market."

"You're selling it?"

He nodded. "This part of my life is over now. We didn't spend a ton of time here anyway. We were on the road most of the time, traveling from one rodeo to the next."

"What about during the school year?"

"My grandmother was a retired teacher, so she homeschooled me."

She wondered again about his parents, but now wasn't the time to drag up what she suspected were bad memories. He had enough to deal with at the moment.

"Do you want to get started now, or do you need some time?"

His gaze connected with hers, and she could see him trying to puzzle out, yet again, why she was here with him.

"Might be good to have something to do," she said.

"You don't have to do anything. You've done more than enough already."

"I don't mind. Honest."

She didn't know if he didn't want to argue with her or if he really just didn't want to face the task of going through the pieces of his grandparents' lives alone, but he finally nodded once.

After they ate, they raided the attic for a few boxes and started dividing up what was going to charity, what was going to the garbage and what Wyatt thought he could sell. They worked for hours, packing, hauling, cleaning. Chloe looked up at one point, enjoying watching Wyatt move.

She was glad to see he was careful of his injuries,

but she could also see improvement every day. That was probably born of the fact that he was used to having to heal quickly so he could get back to work. A shiver went down her spine when she thought of him getting back on a bull. It was a good thing she'd be going home soon because she didn't want to see him injured again, or worse. Seeing the aftermath when she'd barely known him had been bad enough. Having to watch it happen when she was in love with him? She couldn't bear that.

He nearly caught her watching, so she jerked her gaze back to the cabinet below a bookcase. She pulled out some old magazines and had to smile when she found a Scrabble game in a box that had seen better days.

"I see where your affinity for this came from."

Wyatt glanced her way then walked across the room toward her. "It's how Grandma taught me how to spell."

"I think you should keep this."

Wyatt took the box from her and opened the lid. He had a faraway smile as he opened the board. "You up for a game?"

"If you're in the mood to get beat like a drum."

He lifted an eyebrow. "We'll see about that."

As they played the game sitting at his grandparents' little kitchen table, eating pizza they'd ordered, Chloe tried not to think how much she would miss him when she left. Down deep within her, it felt wrong to even think about leaving. Though they still hadn't known each other all that long, being with him felt natural, easy. She'd gotten used to seeing him every day, looked forward to talking to him after a long day at the clinic. And what they'd shared the night before they left Texas, well, an hour couldn't pass without her reliving it and wanting to experience being that close to him again.

Wyatt pecked the edge of the board. "Your turn."

She realized he'd caught her daydreaming. Could he possibly know about what? "Sorry. Guess I'm more tired than I thought."

"There's a cure for that." Wyatt stood and held his hand out to her.

She took it and let him pull her to her feet. He tugged her a little more, right into his arms. In the next moment, his mouth had captured hers. When they finally came up for air, Wyatt wordlessly led her to bed. They didn't make love, but she didn't mind. When he wrapped her in his arms and kissed her forehead, her heart filled with a rush of happiness. As she drifted toward sleep, she knew she didn't want to let this go. Didn't want to let Wyatt go.

WYATT TOOK A few moments by himself at the side of his grandfather's grave to say goodbye. He dreaded the finality of walking away, but he could see the grounds crew waiting to lower the casket and cover it with freshly turned earth.

He'd never been a man to shed tears, but he hadn't been able to help it as the minister performed the short service. He'd heard a few sniffles from the people who'd come to pay their respects—neighbors, long-time friends of his grandparents, staff members from the nursing home and a few familiar faces from area ranches and the rodeo circuit. Even his grandpa's old roping partner, Ernie, was wheeled in by his grand-daughter, Violet.

Through it all, Chloe had been right there as if it

were nothing out of the ordinary for her to help him. Maybe it was just who she was, a person whose heart was so big to counteract all the heartless people in the world, like his parents.

He glanced at the half of the headstone that bore his grandma's name. He wasn't sure what he believed about the afterlife, but he liked the idea of them being together again. His grandpa hadn't been the same man without his other half.

Wyatt glanced over his shoulder toward where Chloe stood next to the parking area talking to Violet and Ernie. Was she his other half? And if so, how cruel fate was.

He turned back toward the grave and placed his hand against the silver casket. "'Bye, Grandpa. Give Grandma a kiss for me, okay?" A lump rose in his throat, and he swallowed hard against it before he turned and headed toward Chloe.

When he reached the others, Chloe took his hand. That connection felt like the most wonderful thing in the world. No, more than that, but he didn't have the poetic words to describe how that simple touch made him feel.

Ernie pointed a gnarled finger at Chloe then glanced at Wyatt. "This one's a keeper. You're going to have to watch her closely or someone will snatch her from you. Just might be me." His mischievous wink and raspy laugh caused Wyatt to smile.

"Don't make me have to wrestle you, old man."

"Wrestle, nothing. I'll just run over you with this chair."

Chloe smiled then leaned forward and kissed Ernie on the cheek. As she stood straight again, she clasped

Ernie's hand. "It was nice to meet you, Ernie. You ever get down to Texas, you let me know and I'll fix you a big batch of Texas barbecue."

Ernie used his other hand to slap the arm of his wheelchair. "Well, what are we waiting for?"

Everyone laughed, chatted for a few more minutes, and then Violet had to get Ernie home to take his medicine.

Chloe seemed to know Wyatt needed quiet on their drive back to the house, but she held his hand the entire time, giving him silent support. He wanted to scream because soon she'd be hundreds of miles away, and he might never see her again.

As he followed her into the house, he fought the urge to tell her how he felt. But how could he be that selfish? He had no idea how he could provide for her. Sure, she had a good job, would always make more than he did. And he didn't begrudge her that. But he'd at least like to be able to give her more than an old pickup that had seen better days, sporadic income and a pile of hospital debt. And she certainly didn't need a mother-in-law who was in prison.

No, he had to let her go *because* he loved her.

When he came out of the bathroom a few minutes later, the dress hanging in his bedroom let him know Chloe had already changed into her casual clothes. He listened but didn't hear her. After tossing the clothes he'd worn to the funeral onto the chair in his bedroom, he went in search of Chloe. He found her sitting at the kitchen table looking at pictures. His heart took a dive when he recognized the photo album.

She looked up at him then lifted one side of the

album so he could see the photos. She pointed toward the photo he should have burned ages ago.

"Is this you? You were a cute little guy."

"Yeah."

Her forehead wrinkled. "Are you okay?"

No, but how was he supposed to explain why? He could tell her the truth. Maybe it would even make it easier when she left.

Yeah, right. The only thing that would make that easier was amnesia.

She glanced back at the picture then closed the album. "I'm sorry if I upset you. I should have asked first."

"No, it's not that." He shifted his focus toward the window, saw a little kid riding a bike down the sidewalk much as he had all those years ago. Damn, the thought of confessing everything to Chloe was way scarier than getting atop a bull that was determined to send him to the dirt. He crossed his arms and forced himself to meet her gaze.

"I don't like seeing pictures of my parents."

"I didn't mean to add to your sadness."

"I'm not sad. Angry is more like it." He took a deep breath, considered stopping before he let the truth out. But the feeling that he owed her the truth settled on him. "I came to live with my grandparents because my parents were arrested and sent to prison."

He expected a look of horror or disgust, but she only showed the slightest change in expression, to sympathy. "What happened?"

He stared at her for a moment before going to stand next to the window to gaze outside. "They were addicted to drugs. Neither of them could hold down a job, so they robbed a convenience store one night to get drug money. The clerk tried to hit an alarm, and my dad shot him."

"Did...did the clerk die?"

The hesitation in her question broke his heart. Was she right now wishing she were back in Texas, far away from him and the ugly truth of his background?

"No, but his life was never the same after that. He's paralyzed from the neck down." Wyatt resisted the urge to punch through the window. "He was just a college kid working his way through school. The irony is that he wanted to be a doctor. Now, he probably wishes he never had to see another doctor as long as he lives."

"That's so sad."

It was more than sad. It was a tragic waste, in so many ways.

"Do you see them?"

"No." He stopped and closed his eyes for a moment when he realized how sharp his answer had been. "My dad died in prison after only a couple of years. I've been to see my mother once."

"Once the entire time she's been there?"

From anyone else, the question would have sounded like an accusation. But with Chloe, he knew it was her innate need to fix and protect others that prompted the question.

"That was enough. She asked me to smuggle drugs into the prison for her. I told her no and that she'd blown her one shot of ever having a relationship with me again." Though he feared what he'd see on Chloe's face, he forced himself to look at her. His heart swelled when he didn't see anger or accusation or even pity, but he knew better than to get his hopes up. "I know it probably disappoints you that I haven't tried again, but I can't. I won't. They were the type of people who hurt everyone around them, even the people who wanted to love them."

He slowly turned to fully face her. "So, there you have it. I'll understand if you want to leave."

She sat still for a few seconds before she slowly stood.

He'd meant what he said. Only he hadn't expected her to want to leave immediately. He could kick himself to Montana and back.

Instead of heading for the door or even the bedroom to pack her things, she rounded the table and came to stand directly in front of him. She placed one hand on his crossed arms and used the other to frame his jaw.

"What your parents did is no reflection on you. You didn't shoot that clerk."

"But—"

Chloe placed her fingers against his lips. "Would you think any less of me if I'd told you my mother was a drunk driver rather than probably being run over by one?"

He looked into her eyes and saw a depth of understanding he'd never seen before. "No."

"No difference."

Where had she been in those dark days before he'd moved in with his grandparents, when the kids at his first school had teased him mercilessly after his parents had been arrested and seemed to appear on the news every night?

In Texas with her loving family, that's where.

Chloe took his hands in hers and rubbed her thumbs over his knuckles. When she looked up into his eyes again, she had such a warm, open expression on her face that he fell the rest of the way in love with her.

"We can't choose our families, but we can pick our friends and who we let into our hearts." She took one of his hands and placed it over her heart. "I choose to let you in, Wyatt Kelley."

Unable to resist any longer, he pulled her to him and kissed her as if the world were ending all around them. Wanting to be even closer to her, he led her straight to bed.

After they made love, he couldn't stop touching her, loving the feel of her soft skin, making sure she hadn't fled during one of the blinks of his eyes.

"You're too good to be true," he said as he skimmed her cheek with his thumb. "Too good for me."

"Now that's just dumb." She scooted closer and dropped a light kiss on his lips.

He caught her hand and held it against his chest. "It's not. I don't have much to offer you."

"If you're talking about material things, I might have to punch you. Do you take me for someone who cares about that?"

"No, but it's a guy thing. We want to be able to take care of the women we love."

Chloe froze, and for a moment Wyatt was afraid he'd said the wrong thing. When a smile started at her mouth and spread to her eyes, he knew it was the best moment of his life.

"So, I'm not the only one who feels this way?"

Wyatt couldn't look away from her face, afraid if he did the truth shining in her eyes would disappear. He realized he'd seen that truth building in her for days but had convinced himself he wanted it so much that he'd imagined it.

"I was probably as scared to admit it as you were," she said.

"Because you didn't know me?"

"Partly. I mean, loving someone is supposed to take time, right?"

"So you're not one of those people who believes in love at first sight?"

"I believe in infatuation at first sight, and that might lead to love."

He grinned at her. "Were you infatuated with me, Dr. Brody?"

She poked his chest with one of her fingers. "Don't get full of yourself, cowboy."

"So you weren't?"

She rubbed where she'd poked him. "You weren't hard to look at."

He lifted her chin. "Neither were you, Doc."

She lowered her eyes. "I was more afraid of what caring about someone would mean. I began wondering if all of us—Dad, my brothers and I—were alone because somewhere deep down we didn't want to get hurt."

"Because of the loss of your mom."

She nodded.

"That's why you've been so concerned about me riding again."

"Yeah. And I'm a doctor, not generally a fan of situations where people put their lives in danger." She lifted her gaze to his. "But yes, I hate the idea of you climbing on a bull, maybe getting hurt again. Or worse. But, I also know that I have no right to ask you to quit.

All I can tell you is that to fully heal, you need to not strain those muscles for a few more months. And they may injure more easily even after you've completed your recovery."

His entire identity felt threatened. But maybe it was time to think about the next stage of his life. Maybe he'd avoided it long enough.

As he pushed a lock of Chloe's hair away from her cheek, he knew that he wanted to find a way to have that next stage include her. He'd been alone most of his life, had always told himself he was fine with it.

He wasn't fine with it anymore.

Chapter Fifteen

"You're going to need some blood-pressure medication," Chloe said as she patted Joan Faris on the hand then began writing the prescription.

"The joys of getting old."

"I know." Chloe ripped the prescription off the pad and gave it to Joan. "But it's better than the alternative."

When Joan left the tent they'd set up on the lawn behind the clinic, Chloe wiped her brow and took a drink of her huge cup of lemonade. She'd been going nearly nonstop all day, barely taking a break to eat a quick lunch from the potluck the local churches had set up under an adjacent tent, which also housed the entertainment meant to keep people occupied while they waited for their turn to see one of the doctors or nurse practitioners.

She glanced out and saw a truck driving by on Main Street pulling a horse trailer. Chances were the driver was headed to the fairgrounds for that night's rodeo. The sight of it caused a pang. It'd been two weeks since she'd left Wyatt in Wyoming because she couldn't put off coming back to work any longer. He'd kissed her at the airport and said he'd see her soon, whenever he got things squared away with his grandfather's estate.

She'd come back to Blue Falls riding high on the knowledge that the man she loved felt the same way about her. But with each passing day, she'd lost a little more of that elation and started to worry when Wyatt began to seem distant during their phone conversations. Now that a thousand miles separated them, had he changed his mind? Had he realized that what he felt for her wasn't love at all but rather gratitude for being there when he needed someone?

Chloe swallowed against the emptiness that was threatening to widen within her again. She needed to stay focused on work and get through this incredibly busy day. There would be time later for sadness and kicking herself for opening herself up to that kind of pain.

She glanced over to where Sophie and Jenna had been directing patients to the appropriate doctors since early that morning. "What do we have next?"

The two nurses shared a quick look between them that Chloe couldn't decipher. Whatever it was, she didn't have time to deal with that, either.

"There's a guy who says he thinks something is wrong with his heart," Sophie said.

With the heat bearing down on the Hill Country today, the last thing someone with a heart problem needed was to be kept waiting. "Show him in."

Chloe turned her back to take another drink as she heard Sophie say, "Right this way."

When Chloe spun to face her newest patient, it was her heart that skipped a beat. "Wyatt." And then what Sophie had said echoed in her head again, and panic hit Chloe right in her middle. "Sophie said something was wrong with your heart." How could that be possible? He was young, healthy.

Wyatt lifted his hand to his heart. "It feels like half of it is missing."

The words were so out of character for him that it took her a moment to realize what he was saying and that there actually wasn't something physically wrong with him.

Wyatt groaned a little. "That's too cheesy, isn't it?"

"No. Just unexpected."

"Yeah, I felt like a giant goof standing in the pharmacy reading all the greeting cards, trying to figure out something romantic to say when I saw you again."

A smile tugged on her lips then grew. "The image of you reading all those cards just might be the most romantic thing I've ever heard in my life."

Wyatt lifted a brow. "Yeah? Good enough to get me a kiss?"

Chloe didn't care who saw her. She ran into his arms and kissed him with all the happiness that was suddenly surging inside her. If she had an entire dictionary's worth of words at her disposal, she wouldn't be able to properly express how good it felt to be held in Wyatt's arms again.

When they finally broke the kiss, she looked up into his eyes and smiled like an idiot.

"I'll have some of what he's having," said a middle-aged guy who was being examined by Dr. Hershel.

That made everyone in the tent laugh, even Chloe as she leaned her forehead against Wyatt's chest. After a moment, he framed her face with his hands and kissed her on the forehead.

"I see you're busy, so I won't hold you up any longer."

She wanted to grab hold of him, irrationally afraid that if he walked out of the tent she'd never see him again. But common sense told her that he didn't drive all the way to Blue Falls just to give her a goodbye-for-good kiss.

"Okay." That single word felt like the bravest thing she'd ever said.

He was gone before she thought to ask him where he'd be. Would he feel comfortable going to the ranch, or would he get a motel room? She considered texting him, but the afternoon proved to be as busy as the morning. From all accounts, the free food, clothing and household items areas were just as busy. She hated seeing that many people in need but so happy that they were being helped. They had Wyatt to thank for that.

She finally finished with the last patient of the day, a shy Hispanic girl named Anna. The little girl finally came out of her shell and smiled when Chloe presented her with one of the miniature stuffed animals she kept on hand for just such occasions. After prescribing antibiotics for the girl's sinus infection, Chloe was caught off guard when Anna wrapped her arms around her in a hug.

As Chloe touched Anna's head and smiled down at her, that ticking clock inside her started tolling like Big Ben. She had no idea where her relationship with Wyatt was going, if anywhere, but she found herself imagining having his children with a clarity that nearly made her stagger.

"You okay?" Jenna asked when the family left the tent.

Chloe nodded. "Yeah. Just wiped out."

"I hear ya. I feel like half the county came through here today."

"Felt like half of Texas."

It took another hour for the staff and volunteers to get all the equipment, files and other supplies back into the clinic. By the time she was finished, all Chloe wanted to do was go home, soak in a bath and then sleep for about twelve hours. Well, that's what she'd want if she didn't feel she had to make an appearance at the rodeo since the proceeds were going to pay for the free clinic they'd just concluded.

And if Wyatt weren't waiting for her.

But when she drove up in front of her house a few minutes later, Wyatt's truck was nowhere to be seen. She shoved down the wave of panic that hit her, telling herself to stop being so ridiculous.

She met Garrett coming out of the house as she was headed in.

"I heard things went well today," he said.

"Yeah."

He nodded. "Mom would be proud."

She smiled at that. "Yeah, I think she would."

When Garrett started to walk away, she asked him, "Has Wyatt been here?"

"No. Is he back in town?"

She detected the note of surprise her brother wasn't quite able to hide. When she'd returned from Wyoming, her dad had been happy for her when she'd told her family how she and Wyatt felt about each other. Owen had been his usual teasing self. But Garrett, he'd been more cautious, doing the protective, big-brother thing.

"He came to see me while I was working."

He didn't respond immediately but then nodded once. "Good. I hope it works out the way you want it to."

As he walked away, she sensed a touch of sadness about him that she suspected had nothing to do with her or Wyatt. As she watched her big brother climb into his truck, she found herself hoping that he could find love one day, too. He was a good man and deserved it.

After she showered and dressed for the rodeo, she checked her phone to see if Wyatt had sent her a message. Her heart leaped when she saw his name on the screen. She touched the screen to open the message.

See you at the rodeo?

She texted back Sure, then did a little dance around her bedroom that would have made a love-struck fifteen-year-old proud.

By the time she got to the fairgrounds, it was already crowded. She scanned the faces she passed on the way from her car toward the grandstand, but none of them belonged to Wyatt. Even looking for a cowboy hat didn't help when she was in a sea of them.

"Hey, Chloe!"

She turned at the sound of Elissa Kayne's effervescent greeting, the one she often used to convince her customers at the plant nursery that they couldn't live without a rose bush or set of butterfly wind chimes. Chloe knew because she'd fallen victim to Elissa's landscaping siren call on more than one occasion.

"Hey, yourself. How are you?"

"Good. You? I bet you're zonked after today. I drove

by and you'd think you were handing out winning lottery tickets."

Chloe supposed that in a way they had been. If not for the free clinic, some of the patients might not have been diagnosed with their conditions in time to have them be highly treatable.

"Fine, but yes, tired." Chloe glanced around. "Where's your more attractive half?"

"Hey! I think I'd be offended if Pete wasn't so darn cute."

"Cute, nothing. He's a hottie."

"You had your chance, missy. It's not my fault no one snapped him up before I did."

Chloe smiled. "Meant to be."

"Yeah." Elissa's smile was full of that newlywed glow, understandable since her wedding to Pete Kayne had only occurred a couple of months earlier. "Speaking of meant-to-be romances, I've been hearing all about your own hunk of cowboy hotness from Verona. Even though I'm not living under the same roof with her anymore, I've been questioning my sanity for letting Pete convince me to live next door."

"You know you'd miss her if you moved farther away."

"Blue Falls isn't that big. Other side of town would have been just fine, even if Pete did already own the property next door." The lot had held Pete's former house for a long time until a tornado the previous spring had blown it off the map. "Oh, and I didn't answer your question. Pete's on patrol tonight."

"How's he liking the switch to state police? Sure seems weird not seeing him working alongside Simon and the guys at the sheriff's department."

"He likes it, but I know he also misses the old job, too. Those guys are like family to him. Now stop avoiding my question. Where's your yummy bull rider?"

"Around somewhere. I'm supposed to meet him here."

"So things are going well?"

Chloe gave a little shrug. "I think so."

Elissa gestured for Chloe to follow her. "Come sit with us. Let Wyatt come to you."

Chloe fought the need to search the crowd until she found Wyatt and followed Elissa to the grandstand. "Us" turned out to be India, Skyler, Keri Teague and several other members of the Teague clan. Higher up, she spotted Jake and Talia Monroe. In front of them, Jake's daughter, Mia, was sitting and chatting up a storm with her best friend, India's stepdaughter, Ginny. Seeing the little girls together made that newly awakened maternal yearning twist inside Chloe.

After several greetings, Chloe took an empty spot next to Elissa and tried watching the events in the arena. But her gaze kept wandering to the crowd, wondering where Wyatt was. She checked her phone and still didn't have a response to the text she'd sent when she arrived. Had Wyatt decided not to come? Should she go home? No, she reminded herself, she was here in an official capacity, too, representing the clinic.

So she told herself to stop worrying, to enjoy talking with her friends and watching the riders compete. She cringed when one of the bareback riders got tossed into the dirt at an awkward angle. That was going to leave some bruises and maybe result in a trip to the chiropractor.

As there was a lull in competition between the bare-back and team roping events, Chloe scanned the crowd again. She was beginning to think that Wyatt wasn't going to show when she spotted him—back behind the pens that held the bulls.

Her heart nearly stopped. Surely he wasn't going to climb astride a bull, not this soon. There was no doubt in her mind that he'd negate all the progress he'd made toward healing completely, might even injure himself worse this time. And he knew that she didn't want to be a witness to that.

She tried to rein in her fear, telling herself there was a logical explanation. But the longer she sat watching him talk to the other cowboys, the more her stomach knotted.

"You okay?"

Chloe glanced at Elissa, who was looking at her with concern. "I don't feel so well. Excuse me."

She hurried down the steps and ran alongside the bleachers, then past the lines extending out from the concession stand, and out into the field where the cars were parked. She could still hear everything the announcer was saying, so she'd know when the rodeo was over and she needed to go make an appearance as the representative of the clinic. But she wouldn't have to watch Wyatt put his life in danger if he were stupid enough to climb atop one of those bulls.

She'd told him she didn't have the right to ask him to quit, and she'd come to terms with loving a bull rider. But this soon, when the risk was even greater? That she couldn't bear to watch.

She lifted her gaze to the stars, thought about her

mom looking down at her all these years. What did she think of Wyatt? Of her daughter finally falling in love?

"Mom, please keep him safe."

WYATT SHOOK LIAM PARRISH'S hand, sealing the deal that would transition Wyatt to a new phase of his life, one he hadn't foreseen before settling astride Beelzebub in this very arena.

"Just call me when Chloe gives you the okay," Liam said. "No way I'm going against doctor's orders, especially Chloe's. She knows where I live."

Wyatt laughed. "Will do, and thanks again."

Liam nodded and went off to deal with some issue that needed his attention as the head of the rodeo company putting on the event.

Left alone, Wyatt wandered over to the back of the pens. He stared at the bulls. They all seemed so calm at the moment, but the moment a cowboy got on their backs they'd become bucking beasts. A pang of loss hit him right in the middle, and for a moment he wondered if he'd made a mistake. But then he remembered that he'd done nothing but think about his decision for the past two weeks as he'd dealt with dispensing with his grandparents' belongings and their home. The longer he'd been away from Chloe, the more he knew what he had to do, wanted to do. It was time for a change. And he'd realized that it was as much for him as for what he might have with her.

As he headed away from the pens, he noticed Owen chatting up one of the barrel racers. Owen glanced over and caught sight of him.

"Hey, look who's back in town."

"You seen Chloe?"

Owen smiled. "And I guess I know why. I saw her earlier sitting in the stands with a bunch of her friends." Owen turned and pointed. "Right there on the end."

"Thanks."

As Wyatt started to walk away, Owen spoke again. "You be good to my sister. Just remember my brother and I have a big ranch, lots of space to hide a body."

Wyatt smiled as he looked back at Owen. "I'll keep that in mind."

When Wyatt reached the grandstand, however, he didn't see Chloe anywhere.

"You looking for Chloe?" He looked up to see a dark-haired woman sitting next to Chloe's friend, India.

"Yeah."

The woman used her thumb to point behind the bleacher area. "She said she wasn't feeling well and went that way."

Concern propelled him toward the restroom area. But after a few minutes of waiting there without seeing her come out, he wondered if she'd gone home. When he reached the edge of the field where all the vehicles were parked, he saw her standing a couple of rows in with her face pointed toward the sky.

"Chloe? You okay?" he asked as he approached her.

She spun around then glanced behind him toward the arena, confusion creasing the area between her eyes. "You're not riding?" She was trying to sound matter-of-fact, but he heard the note of hope, of tentative relief.

He took a couple of slow steps toward her. "No. My doctor says I shouldn't."

She raised an eyebrow. "Since when do you listen to your doctor?"

Another step and he was able to caress her cheek. "Since I fell in love with her."

Again, she directed her gaze toward the arena. He touched her chin and guided her attention back to him.

"I'm not going to be riding bulls anymore."

"You're not? But you said you love it."

"I do, but it's time to step away. It just took me a while to accept that."

"What are you going to do now?"

"Well, right now I was thinking about kissing this pretty girl I know."

"Is that right?"

"Yep." He grabbed her around the waist and pulled her close. And then he captured her mouth with his, kissing her the way he'd imagined in great detail for the past two weeks.

Chloe eventually pulled away. "Not that I'm complaining, but you're avoiding really answering my question."

"Am I?"

She playfully punched him in the shoulder, eliciting a chuckle from him.

"Okay, okay. How would you feel if I decided to make Blue Falls home?"

Her eyes widened in a way that gave him hope that this conversation was going to turn out the way he'd imagined it.

"I wouldn't be opposed to the idea."

He smiled. "Good. Because you're looking at the newest employee of Parrish Rodeo Company."

"That's why you were back behind the pens, talking to Liam?"

"Yes, ma'am. I'll be taking care of the stock and

eventually riding pickup in rodeos, just as soon as my pretty doctor clears me to work."

"That's great!"

"Yeah?"

"Yeah. We're tied with the number of Scrabble wins. I have to have the chance to beat you and proclaim myself the champion."

"Board games? That's really what you're thinking about right now?"

Chloe placed her hand flat over his heart. "No, but what I'm thinking isn't appropriate for a parking lot only yards away from half of Blue Falls."

He lifted a brow. "That right? I might be persuaded to take you to a more appropriate place."

Chloe lifted onto her toes and planted a soft kiss on his lips. "I think that sounds like a very good idea."

They stood kissing for several moments before the need to be alone with her made Wyatt break the kiss. "I really want to sweep you off your feet right now."

"As your doctor, I strongly discourage that."

He ran his thumb over her soft lips. "Guess I'll just have to save that for the day I carry you across the threshold."

Chloe froze and stared at him as if she couldn't possibly have heard him correctly.

"That's right, Chloe Brody, I'm not going to rush you, but I plan to make you my wife someday."

A twitch at the edge of her mouth slowly built into a smile. "You know, Wyatt Kelley, I like your new life plan. I think it's just what the doctor ordered."

And then she kissed him with so much passion that

he thought he might end up right back in the hospital. Not that he would mind as long as he was guaranteed the prettiest doctor in all of Texas.

Epilogue

Chloe nearly choked on her barbecue as Wyatt told the story of the night he'd chased the fence cutters through her family's pasture. Only this time, the recounting he was sharing with a group of their wedding guests included him threatening to lasso the culprits.

"That story gets more crazy every time you tell it," she said.

Wyatt leaned close enough that she could smell his spicy aftershave. "Shh, you're ruining the tale of my heroics."

She smiled. "Oh, pardon me. I thought it was enough that the guys were arrested."

"A little extra embellishment doesn't hurt." Her husband leaned closer and dropped a kiss on her lips.

Her husband. There were moments when she still couldn't believe that an hour ago, she and Wyatt had stood on the front porch of her family's home and said "I do" to each other.

"My eyes!"

Wyatt lifted his lips from hers in time for Chloe to see Owen covering his eyes as if seeing his big sister kiss a guy would burn out his corneas. She grabbed a roll from the basket in front of her and beaned him in the side of the head with it.

Everyone laughed as Owen cried foul. When India's little girl, Rose, started giggling and waving her hands with enthusiasm, that made everyone laugh even more. Even Skyler and Logan's son, Ethan, only two months old, shared a big, toothless grin at the people around him.

Chloe smiled at the little ones and resisted asking their mothers to hold one of them. That maternal instinct had grown even more since Wyatt had returned to Blue Falls with the intent to stay. She wanted to have his children, but she kept telling herself to take things one step at a time. Now she should be enjoying her time alone with Wyatt before bringing kids into the mix, and it would also give him time to adjust to his new life. At least that's what she told herself until she spotted an adorable baby and that yearning inside her kicked into high gear.

"So, has Verona started trying to match up these two yet?"

"Good Lord," Skyler said. "Don't give her any ideas."

"I can see it now, baby matchmaking," Elissa said quietly, scanning the crowd for her aunt. "It's bad enough that she asks me about once a week if I'm pregnant yet."

Chloe caught sight of Verona talking with Greg Bozeman, who looked as if he wanted to make a beeline for his truck. "You know what might cure this?" She smiled. "We should totally set Verona up with someone."

Logan snorted. "That might be the best idea I've ever heard."

As the women started tossing out the names of eligible bachelors near Verona's age, the guys vacated the table in favor of a trip to the iced tubs of beer. Well, they did until the band struck up the first tune. Then they gradually made their way back to claim dances with their wives. Chloe was about to go play with the babies that India and Skyler had put in a playpen when Wyatt pulled her into his arms.

"I think it's tradition for the groom to dance with the bride, isn't it?"

"That's what I hear."

She felt as if her smile consumed her entire face as Wyatt spun her onto the makeshift dance floor. When he pulled her close, she knew she'd never had a happier moment in her life.

"I think I know what to get you for a wedding present," he said.

"Wait, you haven't gotten me anything yet?"

"I was waiting to find the perfect gift."

She laughed. "Yeah, right."

He stared at her with mock affront. "Well, I just won't give you the perfect gift I just thought of."

She swatted him on the chest. "Oh, no, you don't. I'm curious now. What is this perfect gift?"

Wyatt turned his gaze to the left, drawing her attention that way, as well. Her breath caught as she realized the only thing within his line of vision was the playpen. Slowly, she lifted her eyes to Wyatt's.

"Really?"

He lifted his hand and caressed her cheek. "It's obvious you want a baby."

"But what about you?"

"I never thought about it much until I met you, but I like the idea of a little version of you toddling around."

"We can wait. I know we haven't had much time with just us."

"We can have a baby and still manage time for just us." He glanced over the gathering of her friends who were becoming his, as well. "I'd say we have a lot of babysitters at our disposal."

Wyatt paused as a mischievous grin stretched his mouth.

"Oh, dear, I'm afraid to ask what you're thinking."

He pulled her closer and spoke next to her ear. "I'm thinking I'm going to like trying to make that baby."

Warmth flooded Chloe's body as she thought about that, as well. She leaned back so she could meet his gaze. "How soon can we get rid of these people?"

Wyatt laughed and she knew she'd never get tired of hearing that sound, of seeing him smile, of feeling him hold her close. The cowboy in her arms was the perfect prescription for what her doctor's heart needed, and she never planned to let that prescription expire.

* * * * *

Be sure to look for HER COWBOY GROOM,
the next book in Trish Milburn's
BLUE FALLS, TEXAS series,
available in May 2015 wherever books
and ebooks are sold!